OUTLAWS OF AMERICA

JOHNNY ZED.   Life's a winner-take-all game of power. Johnny plays all sides, breaks all the rules—and may hold all the cards...

SHELLY TRACER.   The lethal lover from the deadly streets; she's the ultimate revolutionary—or a high-tech Joan of Arc...

KARL WINSTON.   When is the child father to the man? When a metamorphic killer takes on a human form masquerade...

GRAMMATICA.   The snakeskinned bodyshop sculptor can turn you into a new person. But he'd rather turn you into a beast...

LEE JONES.   Speaker of the House, King of Capitol Hill: this congressman doesn't have constituents. He has slaves...

From the horror-infested Sprawl to grand glittercrowd estates, from the lairs of half-human hunters to the data-pulse of electronic space, the Disruption Revolution is their private war—with the soul of America at stake!

JOHNNY ZED

JOHNNY ZED

JOHN BETANCOURT

POPULAR LIBRARY

An Imprint of Warner Books, Inc.

A Warner Communications Company

POPULAR LIBRARY EDITION

Cover design by Don Puckey
Cover Illustration by Beau and Alan Daniels

Popular Library books are published by
Warner Books, Inc.
666 Fifth Avenue
New York, N.Y. 10103

 A Warner Communications Company

Printed in the United States of America

First Printing: July, 1988

10 9 8 7 6 5 4 3 2 1

The subtle, truly debilitating manifestations of a degenerate society are twofold. First, the ruling class no longer cares for the proletariat. Second, the proletariat no longer cares.

—Joseph S.L. Gilford
Essays from Nowhere

—1—

SHE let Johnny gag her mouth with a belt, that way she wouldn't scream when he amputated her two mangled fingers. The bomb she'd been planting in the turbostation had a bad timer; her fault, she knew, since she'd built it. It detonated two seconds after she'd set it to blow. A flash of light as she closed the locker door, and then little bits of steel ripped into her: face, neck, breasts, hands. Her right hand caught the worst of it. Blood all over her, smoke billowing all around, people hitting the floor and covering their heads, a fat old woman screaming hysterically, her standing there in shock—

Johnny and Karl had hustled her out into their waiting Volkswagen beetle even though she'd left more than enough blood on the pavement for the feet to put a tracer out on her. "Leave me!" she'd screamed then. "*Leave* me, you assholes, I'm feetmeat!" But they didn't. She'd say

1

that for them: though they'd been together only a week, they were loyal to the end.

Now she could hear Karl puking in the motel room's small bathroom. *No stomach*, she thought with disgust. *Some Disruptionist, him! Can't stand a little blood*. She giggled. Then she looked at the sheets on the bed. *Okay, a lot of blood*. She was high on the tail end of a coke lift and couldn't feel a thing.

"Relax," Johnny said softly. "It'll be over in a moment."

"O . . . *ooooooo*ver . . ." The words tasted funny. She giggled.

Johnny Zed just sighed. He bent to his work.

She stared at the yellowed, waterstained ceiling as she listened to the snip of shears and the *sssst!* of a cauterizer. She didn't need the gag. She was tough; she'd lost fingers a dozen times before. Hazard of the job. Still, Johnny had insisted, and when Johnny got some jack-dumb idea into his head there was no getting it out of him.

"Shelly," he said.

"Mmph?" she said back. The bare bulb behind him cast a halo of light around his head. For an instant his face wavered, then it came back into focus. His eyes were glassy, pupils dilated cow-eye big. She didn't know what he was on—he always had custom drugs—and she didn't particularly like the effect this time.

"They're off." He held up something wrapped in red-stained Kleenex. "No problems. We'll get you new ones tomorrow morning."

Suddenly more sober, she pulled the gag from her mouth with her good left hand and tried to spit its taste from her tongue. "Thanks, Johnny, but it's not gonna do me any good now. Those were special . . . custom jobs from Korea. And feet got my blood, man! I can't go walking into a bodyshop now!"

"Relax, Shel. Hey, you're talking to Johnny Zed, right?"

"Yeah. Johnny Zed." Then her vision surged with blue and they were suddenly floating under water. She giggled again. He seemed to be saying something, but his voice was bubbly and distant and she couldn't make out the words. She smelled sweat and blood and puke, and then the blue had everything and she was totally spaced.

Once upon a time the government of the United States of America was based on the doctrine of revolution: that, when people are dissatisfied with the way things are run, they have the inalienable right to rebel and form a new, more perfect government. Abraham Lincoln's decision to fight the Confederate States (the question of human rights aside [and that was never truly the question]) can be seen as the first great blow to our society.

—Joseph S.L. Gilford
Essays from Nowhere

—2—

SHELLY Tracer dreamed the Disruption. Images of violence drifted like ghosts of the past around her: Harran, who'd led her first cell, and Cherub Caesar, and Dog-eye Ruth, all three chopped to bits by knifebullets. She: hot, wounded, animal-panting, crouching in the alley, garbage underfoot, rats bolting ahead and behind, fear like the taste of bad gin in her mouth. Dead now, all dead but her.

They'd burned her left arm off at the elbow. As she lay in the alley's stinking, decaying muck, feeling the pain and shock of the burn, a rat ran across her back. Its claws tore through the fabric of her shirt, each a little hypodermic needling her skin.

She could smell the blood. Her blood. Harran's, which had sprayed all over her face and chest. Cherub Caesar's. Dog-eye Ruth's. She licked her lips and tasted salt. *Poor, dead Harran*. Him, she had loved. She felt only emptiness inside her now, coiled like a snake through her stomach. *What have we done?*

Overhead, aircars buzzed like nasty insects. She tried to swat them.

Jerking her arms, she woke in a clean bed between stiff white sheets that stank of too much bleach. Little wedges of sunlight shone through the closed blinds so she knew it was day. Safe, safe day. No fighting for the moment. She could smell the sourness of her sweat, could taste bile on the back of her tongue. She relaxed. Her heartbeat slowed.

Johnny was already up and moving around the room. She watched him through slitted eyes, reluctant to come out into reality. He went to the mirror and combed his thinning black hair, then finished buttoning his shirt and knotting a thin silk necktie in place: Johnny Zed always had style. Even the toolpouch at his belt dazzled. Idly she wondered what he was like as a lover: strong, she thought, but gentle. To have his arms, like Harran's, around her . . .

After he strapped on his shoulder harness and checked his pistol, he shrugged on his white linen jacket and pulled the bottom three tabs shut. Then he started for the door.

"Ditching me?" she said, sitting up. A sharp pain behind her eyes made her wince.

"You know me better than that," he said, hand on the knob.

"I wouldn't blame you. You should've ditched me last night. I'm bad for you now that feet got my blood."

"It's nothing that can't be handled."

"What's the latest word?"

"Last I heard was 'Elections.'" He smiled, then, looking young and innocent.

She liked him that way; she wished he smiled more. *Elections*. Yeah, she'd heard that one already.

Then Johnny's mask of calm returned and he seemed a stranger. He said, "Karl went out. He didn't come back."

Suddenly cold inside, she sat up. "How long?"

"Six hours. Something's happened to him. I was going to try a look at the nets, see if anything's up."

"Shit." *The bastard ditched us*.

"Get dressed and we'll get out of here."

She slid out of bed. She was naked and she supposed Johnny'd put her to sleep like the proper gentleman he was. No, he would never touch her uninvited: his charm again, his manners, like a curtain that would always separate them. Her right hand, she saw, was plasticked up so well she couldn't tell where her two stubs ended and the fake fingers began. Her other wounds had been similarly disguised.

"You packed?" she said, quickly going to her Simsung bag and pulling a fresh daysuit from under the various explosives, guns, knives, leaflets, and bundles of bogus thousand-dollar bills. Faster still she pulled the suit on and ran the Velcro tabs shut.

"Yes," he said. He took a scuffed leather suitcase from the top shelf of the closet.

Shelly zipped her bag shut and grabbed its handles with the wrong hand, found all her fingers wouldn't move to grasp it and switched hands with as much grace as she could muster under the circumstances. Then Johnny opened the door for her and she pushed out ahead of him into a long corridor with a dirty, worn carpet on the floor. It might have been blue once; she couldn't tell. Fluorescent lights flickered overhead and numbered doors opened to the left and right. At the far end of the hall stood a grimy window through which she could see the tops of skyscrapers. At least they hadn't left the Sprawl.

"How could you let him go?" she demanded. "You saw the way he was last night, puking his guts out in the sink."

"I saw. He said he had a personal errand and that he'd be back in a few hours. He's done it before."

"After a botched job?"

Johnny shrugged.

"How could you let him go?" she said again.

"We're close, him and me."

"You *were*," she said. He didn't answer. She faced him. "Come on, Johnny, admit it. He's either turned us in to the feet or ratted to the next cell up. Either way, someone's gonna be after us. Shake it loose. We gotta get out of here."

She started for the door marked Fire Exit. Anyone coming after them would use the elevator: an advantage of being near the top floor.

Johnny reached the door first and pushed it open for her.

"There's no need to help me," she said. "I can still manage doors with one hand."

He just grinned that jack-dumb grin of his. "I'm checking for traps before I go out, Shel. I know you wouldn't want me to get hurt."

She paled when she realized what he meant. "Shit."

After making sure there were no traps around the door, she went up the stairs: first two at a time, then one at a time after she'd passed eight floors and started getting winded. By the time she reached the roof exit, her heart beat like a drum in her chest and she was gasping for air.

Johnny took it all in stride. He wasn't even sweating.

The door said ALARM WILL SOUND WHEN OPENED. Johnny squatted down and found the wires, detached them, closed them off with a bit of red electrical tape from the pouch at his belt. Then he pushed the door open, motioned her forward, then laughed when she shook her head. He went out first, into hazy morning sunshine.

Over the tarred roof, straight ahead thirty blocks, she could just make out Billy Penn's statue atop the old Philadelphia City Hall. They'd held some kind of government meetings there back when such things still made sense, back before the Sprawl of Washington-Baltimore-Philadelphia had come into existence. That statue gave her a fix on where they were: somewhere around Fortieth and Chestnut, in the Sprawl's upper-class slums. Johnny'd done good to bring her here. Since few feet bothered to patrol this area, it was right for hiding out.

Johnny set his suitcase down and took a small black box she'd never seen before from his pouch. After folding several solar panels out of its side and angling it toward the sun, he keyed something into the numberpad on its surface. A moment later the speaker cackled with static.

"Yeah?" a woman's voice said.

"This is Gilford," Johnny said. "What's today's word?"

Gilford? Shelly stared at Johnny Zed in surprise. He motioned her to stay quiet. Gilford was their leader, boss of the Disruptionist movement, and for Johnny to impersonate him was tantamount to treason. Shelly bit back her protests, though. He was trying to keep them from getting killed—a goal she heartily supported.

"Representation," said the woman's voice.

"'Representation.' Good; it fits. Now I want last night's report."

"Gimme a minute," the voice said. More static. "Got it here. Twelve-B: mission accomplished. Twenty-three-A: mission accomplished. Twenty-seven-A: mission failed." Twenty-seven-A—that was their cell's number. Shelly swallowed, straining to hear the next words: "No report on Twenty-seven-A since sixteen hundred last night." More static. "Feet got the blood of at least one cell member. Recommendation: disband cell."

Disband. Shelly felt shaky suddenly and grabbed Johnny's arm.

He jerked away from her. "Recommendation denied.

Await Twenty-seven-A's report. Gilford out." Snapping shut the solar panels, he turned on her and glared. "Don't ever do that again, Shel!"

"What?" She looked at him blankly.

"I almost dropped the goddamn phone, and that would have screwed everything!"

"Sorry." Deliberately, she changed the subject. "You said you were Gilford."

"Yes. So?"

"So he's gonna find out! Then he *will* have us disbanded!"

"I doubt it. The last I heard, he was in Geneva meeting with SecurNet negotiators—trying to get back our right to vote for members of Congress, I believe."

"Then they'll know it wasn't him on the phone for sure!"

He shook his head. "We're a bureaucracy, too, Shel. They'll never think to check."

"Shit," she said, realizing all of a sudden the full implications of what HQ'd said. Karl hadn't reported to them. That meant he must've gone running to the feet. *Never trust a man who can't stomach the sight of blood.* She said: "We gotta get out of here. Place'll be swarming with feet any minute—"

Again he shook his head. "They would've been here by now if Karl turned us in. And remember, they're after him as much as they're after us."

"Maybe he bargained?"

"Not his style."

"How do you know so goddamn much about him?" she demanded.

"That's not important. Look, Shel, I'm going after him. If it's humanly possible, I'll get him back. I want you to go to Lightning Statue and wait till midday pickup. Tell them Karl shot himself cleaning his gun, or he gashed his throat open shaving—anything. Get me more time."

"You're gonna track him down and kill him?"

"Just go."

"You're not ditching me." She said it automatically, then didn't know why. After all, what did she owe Karl? She'd known him all of a week, during which they'd carried out three bombings of congressional trains, a teargas attack on a senator's office, and a raid on a government propaganda publisher's files: hardly enough to make her want to risk her life for him. It went against one of her basic rules of life: survival first. She cared about herself, the Disruption, and the members of her cell—in that order. Or so she tried to believe.

Louder, half-disbelieving, she said, "I *am* going with you."

"Why?"

"You and Karl didn't ditch me last night. Maybe I owe you something."

He snorted.

"Why are *you* going after him, then?"

He looked at her. "Karl's my brother," he said.

She didn't know what to say so she just stared up at the sky. *Brothers.* Hell, she never would've suspected. They'd never mentioned it in her presence, never acted like more than friends. They hardly even resembled each other: Johnny was tall and lean, with dark hair and blue eyes; Karl was more heavily built, with ash-blond hair, and pale, icy eyes. Still, she had no reason not to believe Johnny, so she just nodded.

Brothers. Why were things always so complicated?

Johnny didn't waste any time trying to flag a cab. He took a spiderweb-thin flasher from his billfold and unfolded it to its full meter-square size. It activated as soon as he touched the red dot in the corner, blinking red-blue, red-blue, red-blue over and over again. Any empty cab that saw it would come for them.

Shelly sat knees-to-chin and prepared for a long wait: there weren't many aircars out, cabs or otherwise. Johnny sat beside her, folding up those long legs of his into a yoga position. He relaxed visibly, letting all the tension drain from his body. She hadn't realized how keyed he was. Karl really had him worried.

"How come you never said he was your brother?" she asked.

"It didn't seem to matter until now."

"Maybe it didn't. But I don't like the idea of you two keeping secrets from me. We're supposed to be a team, working together for the Disruption. Makes me realize how little I really know about you both."

"Yeah," he said. "You're right. We should've talked— *will* talk, later, after we get him back."

"If Karl didn't run to the feet, then where the hell *did* he go?"

"Home," Johnny said. There was a flatness to his voice she didn't like. She'd never seen him like this before. "He went to check on our mother. He's like that. Father must've seen him come in."

"So?" she prodded.

"Father's in Congress. He'd turn Karl and me over to the police if he ever found us. He knows we're Disruptionists."

"I'm sorry."

"Yeah." He spat. "We've got to get him back. I'd never forgive myself if the police repatriated him."

"Gilford would disband our cell. I don't want to end up working an office."

"That, too."

She leaned back. This was a lot to think about, suddenly.

And suddenly she didn't feel safe close to Johnny Zed. His father in Congress! Shit. That could lead to bad, bad trouble. She thought of ditching him, wished she could, knew she wouldn't. *Dumb*, she called herself. *Real grade-A, jack-prime dumb*.

She cursed helplessly.

There are those who say revolution is dead in this modern age. Perhaps that is true. If so, then we are surely doomed to failure. But I trust that last, hidden spark of humanity, that tiniest byte of conscience and morality, to be my salvation— and the salvation of us all. Awake, ye masses, awake! See the world spreading like a bleak cancer! Take notice! What have we wrought? *What have we wrought?*

—Joseph S.L. Gilford
The Waiting Room

—3—

AN hour later, a cab dropped down from the sky like a wounded bird. It was the oldest aircar Shelly had ever seen in service, with its side bashed in from thrown bricks and its windshield cracked in a dozen different places. Still, its repeller fields shimmered with power and she could hear the steady thrum of its engine. It hovered a foot from the tar roof while its young black driver gave them the once-over.

At last he touched something in the forward compartment and the side hatch sprang open. Johnny scooped up his flasher and suitcase and climbed in first. Shelly tossed her bag in and slid next to him. The door swung shut and clicked locked by itself.

"Careful with that," Johnny said, touching her bag as though it might explode at any moment.

"I'm always careful," she said.

"Where to, man?" the driver asked through the steel mesh grate between them. He started the meter running and its ticker sounded like a watch gone mad. Shelly looked at numbers rolling on the cost screen. They were paying ten newdollars every three seconds: illegally high, but she wasn't going to complain. Just finding a cab here was miracle enough.

Johnny pretended not to notice the meter, either. He said: "Just head for the Delaware. I'll give you directions as we fly."

"Right-o!" Whistling cheerfully, the driver shifted the repeller fields and they shot forward like a bullet from a rifle.

Twenty minutes and quite a few turns later, they landed in an empty baseball field near an abandoned warehouse district. Shelly had lost her bearings long ago: she just knew they were north of Billy Penn's statue, perhaps as much as fifty miles north.

"Call it two thousand four hundred, counting my tip," the driver said, turning and grinning. His teeth had all been filed down into sharp points.

"Call it three thousand," Johnny said, "and forget you ever saw us." He pulled a wad of bills from his pocket and peeled off three crisp new thousands.

Shelly closed her eyes for an instant, wincing inwardly. The money was fake—part of their job was to pass it and disrupt the economy—and she was certain the driver would catch on. People like him were seldom fooled. But he barely glanced at the bills before tucking them into his pocket.

The door unlocked and opened. She stepped out into hot, fresh air and breathed deeply: none of the center-

Sprawl smog here. Johnny Zed followed with both their bags. He handed hers over with almost reverent care.

The aircar took off, repellers raising a thick, choking cloud of dust. Engine roaring, it shot off to the right. In seconds it disappeared behind the warehouses.

"This way," Johnny said, starting toward left field at a good pace. Shelly had to jog to keep up with those long legs of his.

He led her to an abandoned warehouse with a large docking bay in back. The thick Durasteel double doors had long ago been blasted open and now hung at crazy angles. After wading through the trash in the doorway, they found themselves in a long, wide, dimly lit room filled with smashed packing crates and rotted pressboard boxes. The air stank of dust and mold; Shelly didn't like it, not at all.

Johnny just nodded, though. "This'll do."

"Nobody's been here since the riots."

"You'd be surprised." He set down his suitcase, thumbed the lock, and flipped back the top. She saw rows of hitech marvels packed in bubblebags: slamjams, clockers, snake-eyes, lots of things she couldn't identify— enough illegal hardware for the feet to put them both away for more centuries than they'd live years. That stash had to have taken Johnny quite a while to put together.

Shelly opened her Simsung bag, dumped everything out, and took inventory. Eight hundred thousand in counterfeit newdollars, a pair of black daysuits, makeup, hair dye, four throwing knives, six handguns, two boxes of ammo, various plastic explosives, and a padded box containing six eggshell teargas bombs they'd been planning to set off at Senator Dale's birthday party next week. She lined everything up, stared at it a minute, then put it all back except for the teargas bombs and her custom .38 automatic. She didn't think she'd need anything else.

"Dye your hair black," Johnny Zed said suddenly.

"Why?"

"My father's mistresses always have black hair—a hangup of his. If anyone sees you, you might get an extra second or two that way."

It sounded reasonable. She took out her bottle of Black Dye #5 and handed it to him. "You do it. I've only got one hand."

He poured a liberal portion onto her short blonde hair and rubbed it in. She smelled something sweet, like lilacs, as the dye did its job, and her scalp grew warm and tingly beneath his fingers.

"Done," he said at last, wiping his hands on a small white cloth.

She shook her head and felt her bangs shift back and forth. Good: dry already. They could leave. Standing, she kicked trash over their bags. If anyone came in, she didn't want them stealing her equipment.

"Let's go," Johnny said.

A fifteen-minute walk put them beyond the empty, echoing warehouses and into a rich residential neighborhood. Shelly knew it was rich because the paved streets suddenly became neatly mowed strips of green grass. The large row-houses that appeared at either side were well kept, with fresh coats of paint and intricate woodwork all over. On the roofs sat large, shiny new aircars; people here didn't use ground vehicles for anything.

They got a few curious glances from people moving about in rooftop garages, but Shelly ignored them. Johnny was dressed okay for the burbs, with his tie, but she knew she looked bad. Real bad. Usually she couldn't tell, even with a mirror, but this time she *knew*. She wished she'd at least put on a tie.

Johnny touched her hand, startling her. "We're almost there."

"Yeah." Shrugging, she followed him around the corner. A block ahead stood an isolated house, large and ramblingly Victorian, with a ten-foot-high stone wall around it. Bottles had been set in cement atop the wall, then broken to leave jagged, knifelike edges. Stuck on the blades of glass were two weather-grayed human skeletons. Little bits of a faded red dress still clung to one. Shelly studied them with grim amusement.

"They're not real," Johnny said. "Father had them put there after the Riots of '33."

"I figured," she said. "Pleasant."

"Effective."

They walked up to the fence, followed it to the left until they came to a steel gate. A handpad had been set in its middle. As she watched, impatiently glancing left and right, Johnny palmed it. Something hummed deep inside like a hive of bees—but nothing else happened.

Johnny cursed. "They must've changed the locks."

Shelly didn't say word one; nothing she could add would've helped. Johnny was their cell's technical boy, after all. If he couldn't get in, nobody could.

He unhooked the tool pouch from his belt and spread it open on the pavement at his feet. Crouching, he took several bits of metal from a small plastic case and screwed them together into what looked like a malformed screwdriver. A four-pronged needle stuck out instead of a blade, and Shelly could see little blue-white sparks jumping from point to point.

"What's that?" she asked.

"Brainjack."

She'd heard of them but had never seen one in use before. Nobody talked about them much, since they made good businessmen nervous—and that was bad for the economy. Brainjacks were smarter than handpads. When you plugged one in, it would override the pad's programming and add your handprint into memory. Very illegal.

"Hurry," she said, glancing left and right.

After boring a hole in the corner of the handpad with a small drill, Johnny stuck the tip of the brainjack through and fished around inside for a moment. Then he pushed the needles in as far as they'd go, released the handle, and wiped his hands on his pants. The brainjack's monitor flashed green.

"Done," he said. He packed up his tool pouch and hooked it back onto his belt. The whole operation had taken less than a minute: impressive.

He palmed the handpad. This time after the hum came a series of little clicks as tumblers began falling into place.

"Try not to look so nervous," he said, studying her.

"But a congressman's house!"

"My father's house."

She shook her head. Slowly, the gate opened. Johnny entered first this time and she followed almost on his heels. Five seconds later the gate closed again. The lock's click reminded her of a pistol being cocked.

From the other side of a wall came a hiss as the brainjack shorted itself out and burned the gate's memory. It wouldn't do, she thought, to let the feet get Johnny's handprint. Hell, their having her blood was bad enough.

They stood on a winding cement path with fruit trees on both sides. Rows of tall, flowering bushes shielded them from the house's first-floor windows.

Now she heard noise from ahead: the babble of talk, some voices gruff, one half-hysterical, one soothing. And then came a sharp *crack* and a cry of pain that could only have come from Karl.

She felt sick inside and glanced at Johnny. He'd stopped and begun to tremble a bit, like a hound about to be loosed

on a hunt. His cheeks were very white. They got that way
when he was angry—really angry, as if he wanted to kill
someone. She'd only seen him that way once before, when
a congressman they'd been trailing spat in the face of a
beggar.

Smoothly, in one quick motion, Johnny drew his gun.
He started to the left, following the row of bushes, heading
for the house.

"Johnny," she whispered, chasing him. "Wait!"

He looked back at her. "This isn't your affair," he said.
"You can still leave, if that's what you want."

"Hell, no. Shit, Johnny, I came this far—I mean . . . just
wait, okay? Don't go running off. Let's get closer, see
what's happening, then decide what to do."

He smiled a bit. "I didn't think you'd let me down."

"Then you're a bigger fool than I thought you were."

"I know you better than you know yourself, Shel. You
try to be hard, but you can't be because of one fatal flaw in
your character."

She crouched and set down the box of teargas bombs,
looking up at him all the while. "And what's that?" she
said sarcastically.

"You care too much."

She didn't deign to answer. Let him think she cared;
what did it matter? When it came down to looking after
herself, she knew she'd do a good enough job. She always
had before.

Then why am I here? she wondered. She didn't have an
answer. She didn't want to think about it—wouldn't think
about it.

She flopped on her belly and snake-crawled under the
bushes toward the distant voices. Behind her, Johnny did
the same.

It didn't take long to get to where they could see the
front of the house. Two feet aircars sat there, heavy, black,

armored things that only a missile could bring down. In the back of one sat Karl. He was slouched over so the side of his head touched the window. His face had been messed up—bashed with the butt of a rifle. She winced. Messy; she'd seen too many wounds like that before.

Six blue-uniformed feet, four men and two women, stood talking to a tall, thin, gray-haired man in a three-piece suit. On the ground behind them sat a middle-aged woman, her face hidden in her hands: Karl and Johnny's mother, Shelly guessed. The woman's shoulders shook with sobs.

Shelly could feel Johnny next to her, trembling. Tapping his arm, she got his attention. She motioned him back the way they'd come and he nodded. They crawled out from under the bushes and stood, her brushing the dirt and dead leaves from her clothes, him just cursing softly to himself.

"Shut up, will you?" she said, when he began to repeat himself.

"I'll take them from the right; you take the left." He snapped off his pistol's safety.

"Too dangerous. They outgun us, Johnny, and someone'll get killed if we try to take them. There's got to be a better way."

"What, then?" he demanded.

She didn't know; Karl was the one who'd choreographed their raids and strikes, and before him in her previous cell it had been Harran. Both men had done very, very good work. So good she'd never needed to think out any plans for herself. Now she half-wished Karl were here and Johnny the one they were trying to rescue—but then they might not have even gotten through the gate. That was the problem with teams: they fell apart without key members.

Everything she thought of now sounded stupid: posing as maid (they'd all recognize her immediately), gardener (same problem), Avon lady (nobody had let her in). Who got into estates like this except the owners, staff, and feet?

It came to her suddenly: the owners' secret lovers. And she had black hair, as had all of Johnny's father's mistresses. It was all very convenient. They couldn't have planned it better a month in advance.

She could tell from looking at Johnny that he wouldn't be much good in a fight. He looked shaken, uncertain, no longer the decisive leader. She realized she'd have to get Karl out by herself if she didn't want anyone getting killed.

She slipped out of her clothes as Johnny Zed stared, bewildered. She found her mirror compact and brushed on makeup until she looked passably human. Then she selected two of the egg-shaped teargas bombs and cupped them in her hands. It made the stubs of her amputated fingers ache, but she'd put up with worse before: this was for the Disruption more than for Karl or Johnny, and she'd give her whole right leg for the cause. The bombs cupped in her palms probably wouldn't show, she thought, but if they did, she'd count on her tits to distract the feet.

"What's your father's first name?" she asked.

"Sandy. But—"

"Nobody at your house knows me," she said. "I'm going to walk up and create a distraction. As I do that, you circle around and cover me from the other side. In the confusion we'll get Karl out."

"No, absolutely not. It's too risky. You could get—"

But she'd turned and started walking toward the voices by then. She knew that if she waited, he'd talk sense into her and they'd never get Karl out.

"Shit," she heard him say at her back. She just smiled and started to walk her sexiest walk.

It didn't take her long to clear the bushes. The two aircars still sat there, and the six feet still stood talking to

Karl's father. On the ground behind the feet wept Johnny's mother.

It was hard for Shelly to think of Johnny Zed as having parents. It was harder still to believe what she was doing for him and Karl. She swallowed, then put on a radiant smile and stepped out from behind the bushes.

At once the feet whirled and drew their guns. Then they hesitated. Two lowered their pistols, silly grins spreading across their faces. The other four seemed less certain.

"Yoo-hoo, Sandy!" she called. "Where did you put my clothes, dear? I can't find them anywhere!"

She started forward again and that settled it: the feet all reholstered their pistols. The men nudged each other, grinning. The women looked alternately amused and embarrassed. All watched her swaying hips and breasts, not her hands.

Johnny's mother was on her feet now, face red. She turned and began shrieking incoherently at her husband, who tried to interrupt her flow of invective and couldn't. Shelly caught a few of his words: ". . . Never seen her . . . probably the gardener's . . ."

And then she was in the middle of the feet. One of the men had doffed his jacket and was offering it to her. She smiled at him and winked. Then she threw the bombs.

They exploded at once, sending great roiling clouds of gas into the feet's faces. Shelly held her breath and ran for the aircars. Behind her, she heard the helpless gasping and wheezing.

The aircar door stood open. She dove through, pulling it closed behind her. An instant later she heard muted popping sounds and the thick glass window to her left suddenly had three bullets buried in it. She smiled through the fracture cracks as she turned the key and sent the repeller fields running with power. Where the hell was Johnny Zed?

She looked at the bushes but didn't see him. Then she cursed and knew he'd ditched her. She thumbed the lift button on the steering wheel and the aircar rose with a roar. Gunning the engine, she shifted the power fields toward the rear. The car leaped forward. In seconds, they were heading south at 180 kilometers per hour.

The feet would be after them in minutes. Johnny'd ditched her. She was naked and her partner unconscious. She couldn't think of a worse situation to be in.

Karl stirred. "Shel . . . ?"

At least he was awake. "Yeah, it's me. Take it easy, Karl."

"Where . . . what happened?"

"Your brother and I rescued you."

"Who?"

"Me and your brother. You know, Johnny."

He shook his head. "What are you talking about? Johnny Zed's not my brother."

And suddenly she thought of a worse situation.

They say any change in the government is impossible, and any hopes for change insane. Am I insane? I think not. And yet, still I hope.

—Joseph S.L. Gilford
Essays from Nowhere

—4—

S HE turned to look at Karl. "What did you say?"

"Johnny's not my brother."

"Shit. That's what I thought you said." She'd been used, she knew then. Having her dye her hair, tricking her into rescuing Karl by herself—Johnny Zed had planned it all. She didn't like that, not one bit. They were supposed to be a team. But *why* had he done it? What could Johnny hope to gain? *I know you better than you know yourself,* he'd said. What did that mean?

"What's the word?" Karl whispered, distantly.

"Representation." In the mirror, she saw him smile. And then his eyes closed and he seemed to be sleeping.

They were over abandoned warehouses now. She cut their speed and they dropped lower, cruising, looking like just another feet aircar on the prowl. The buildings to either side seemed bleak and lonely, their smashed-out windows black, peering eyes.

Representation. Retaliation would be a better word, doubly apt now. She wanted retaliation not only against the feet and Congress for all they'd done to her country, but against Johnny Zed for lying to her, for using her, for ditching her. Her fantasy of making love to him came back for a second . . . his taut body against her, stroking her, only this time as she saw herself arching her back and thrusting her tongue into his mouth, she also buried a shiv hilt-deep into his side.

Would his blood taste like Harran's? Their eyes would be the same—startled as they died, unsuspecting, Johnny's innocently deep, Harran's just as deep but guilty as hell.

No, she knew then, *I cannot kill him.* It would be too much like watching Harran die again. But she could hate him, oh yes, hate him for what he'd done. And she would never trust those innocent blue eyes again.

Just ahead she saw the place they'd ditched their gear. She guided the aircar up the loading bay, between the blasted-open Durasteel doors, into near-darkness. When she shut off the engine, a depressing silence settled around them.

Karl moaned a bit. She crawled over the seat to see about his wounds.

His hands had been cuffed behind his back and blood ran down the side of his face from a jagged cut just below his left eye. His cheeks were swollen and already blue-black from burst capillaries. She couldn't do much for him now: he needed a bodyshop. But at least the feet didn't have a sample of his blood.

She climbed out and retrieved her bag, then put on one of her black daysuits. Her right hand throbbed. She looked at it and saw the two fake fingers had crumpled a bit— they were cosmetic, after all, and not built for real strain.

Little red lines radiated from the cauterized stubs. She pulled the fingers off and threw them into the trash on the floor, knowing they wouldn't fool anyone anymore.

Then she ripped a sleeve from her spare daysuit and wiped the blood from Karl's face with it. Afterward she bandaged him up as best she could with strips of cloth torn from one of the legs. Johnny had a supply of plastiflesh in his suitcase, but she didn't bother to take it: with Karl's cheeks swelling the way they were, she knew she wouldn't be able to disguise his injuries—they'd only look worse.

The aircar's ignition key, she discovered, also opened the front storage compartment. Inside on hooks dangled several keys, each labeled with a small white tag. One tag said HANDCUFFS—SPARE.

Sure enough, that key opened Karl's cuffs. His wrists had bright red rings around them where the metal had bitten into his flesh. Shelly stretched him out across the whole back seat, putting his hands on his chest and cushioning his head on the remains of her daysuit. She checked his eyes but couldn't tell whether he was in shock. He didn't respond when she called his name or shook his shoulder.

Damn, she thought, *have to get him to a bodyshop fast.* She went out and looked over their stolen aircar.

Yellow insignia on the top and sides branded it as feet property. She'd have to cover that up, she knew, to have a chance of getting into the Sprawl unnoticed. She retrieved the Black Dye #5 from her bag and smeared it over the insignia.The liquid dried almost instantly. It took three coats and the color didn't quite match the aircar's black paint, but when she stood back and finally couldn't see any of the feet markings, she decided it would do.

She stored away her Simsung bag and Johnny Zed's suitcase, climbed in, started the engine, and forced herself to head for the Sprawl at a leisurely pace . . . just like any burber out to shop.

It was a bad day: she saw that even before they made downSprawl, where factories puffed smoke and steam and the residue of a technical society into the air. A heavy chemical haze hung over most of the city here, and from high up it made the tallest buildings into mist-shrouded faery towers from history tapes. Shelly knocked the filters up to high and let cool air blow on her face as she drove.

Soon she dropped down fifty meters, then twenty-five, so the aircar glided between the buildings. Soot-blackened brick and granite and glass slipped by to either side. Transit platforms moved around them, each huge, winged monster carrying several hundred people. Neon from roof signs lit up the haze, made it glow in blue-red-purple splotches as ugly and colorful as the bruises on Karl's face.

"Bodyshop, bodyshop," she whispered to herself, trying to think of the safest of the dives that dealt in human anatomy. She usually frequented Hanging Charlie's, the Ritz of the humanoform boutiques, where the best of anything could be had for the right price: new eyes, new hearts, whole new bodies, even, if you had the cash. She'd gotten her Korean fingers there, and her Japanese eyes, and her Canadian Flexisteel ribs. Problem was Hanging Charlie'd gone legit: since the feet had her blood, she couldn't see him about her wounds. And her fingers were really hurting now.

"St. Jude Street!" she said suddenly. She remembered a lover from long ago, Cal, yes Cal, who had burned out and gone the way of all burnouts. Cal with his dog-whiskered face and nightsight eyes, Cal who had brought her into her first bodyshop and paid for her first new set of fingers. And Cal who had seduced her into the Disruption.

She recalled him talking about a certain back-alley shop off St. Jude Street, one that dabbled in animals' bodies and asked no questions for certain *other* services. They were probably expensive as hell, but they'd be able to help Karl. And her. After all, she had eight hundred kay in fake new-dollars: enough to buy a whole new right arm, practically.

They'd almost reached St. Jude Street, so she began looking for a place to park. Through clots of haze she could see the congested street level swarming with blue-shirts and ground vehicles, hucksters and whores. Hardly enough room remained to walk, let alone land an aircar.

Behind her, Karl groaned and shifted.

"Easy," she called. "Almost there."

A shining glass-and-chrome building jutted out in front of her. It had an aircar port, very slick, very private, and she drove inside without a moment's hesitation. The windshield crackled with blue and yellow lines of electricity as they cleared the smoguard and glided up a ramp into the garage proper. Most of the parking slots had shimmer-screens up around them: twisting shields of silver-colored light that hid from view whatever lay inside. The few air-cars visible ran to the luxury models, bristling with mini-microwave dishes and custom weapon systems, costly hitech toys for upper-class children.

She pulled into an empty slot. The engraved platinum nameplate overhead said: JULIAN ARDENT. She'd never heard of Julian, but his last name belonged to one of the lesser congressional families. Rich, though, very rich— but then it took a lot of money to buy even a small seat in Congress.

A recording droned outside, the flat voice all but lost through the aircar's thick hull: "You have parked in the wrong space. Please remove your vehicle at once. You have parked in the wrong space. Please . . ."

Shelly opened the door and slipped out. "We're friends

of Julian's," she said to the wallspeaker. "He told us we could use his slot today."

The recording cut off suddenly and a woman spoke: "Look, we don't have you scheduled. I'm going to admit you, but tell Mr. Ardent that if he doesn't start phoning his guests in ahead of time, we're going to start throwing them out. And I mean it! Five unscheduled guests in one week is just too many!"

"Sorry," Shelly said. "I'll tell him."

"Be sure you do." And then the speaker cut off amid hisses and crackles of static.

They'd been lucky . . . but then, she knew she could've talked them into the garage anyway. She'd done it before in other places. As long as it looked legit, most attendants didn't care. And anyway, even if they called Julian Ardent to check, she'd still be out of the place before the feet could get there.

She pulled out the luggage, then unlocked the back door and opened it. Karl looked up at her blearily.

At least he's conscious again, she thought. She hadn't been looking forward to carrying him into the bodyshop.

"Can you walk?" she asked.

"I—uh—think so. . . ."

"Good." She steadied his arm as he climbed out. When he tried to straighten up, he doubled over suddenly, gasping. "Careful!" she said, easing him to the cement floor. He leaned up against the aircar, face gray, trembling, arms pressed tight to his left side.

"Broken ribs?" she asked.

He nodded.

"We'll get Flexisteel replacements, too, then."

Karl shook his head. "Don't want those."

"Don't give me that 'natural body' shit. I don't have time for it, and neither do you."

"But—"

"I risked my neck for you. Least you could do is be grateful."

"I meant I—I *am*. Help me up?"

She slung her bag over her shoulder, hefted Johnny's suitcase—it was surprisingly light—then took Karl's arm and pulled him to his feet. He winced but draped his arm around her shoulder. Shelly took most of his weight and managed to get him moving at a quick pace

Just as they reached the lift, its shining steel doors slid open. Two tall, almost emaciated men stepped out. One wore fur skintights of black, the other fur skintights of gold. The front of their heads had been sculpted into ever-smiling cat faces; only their slitted eyes moved. Both shifted cat-soft and cat-quick, hyped on doubletime, and there was something odd about the joints of their legs, their hands, their necks.

They flowed circles around Shelly and Karl, wary, eager. Dropping down, they moved on all fours, like real cats, and Shelly saw their tails, long and sleek, lashing back and forth. She tensed as sharp ivory claws slid from their hands, those curious hands with stubby little fingers.

"Vallis, Dave, that you?" Karl said, almost doubled over from pain.

One of the catmen laughed: a grating purr of a sound, too hard and too high-pitched.

Shelly felt Karl relax a bit in her arms, and she whispered to him, "You know these pussies?"

"They're old friends of mine."

The catman on the left, the old one, leaped forward suddenly, spinning fur and claws, almost too fast for Shelly to follow. She felt a sharp stab of pain across her stomach. Then he was past and bounding away—his legs, she saw now, had been shortened, restructured to match a panther's.

She looked down. Her daysuit had three parallel rips just

below her breasts. Something glistened darkly on the cloth. She touched it, saw it was blood. A tremor ran through her. She tensed, felt her adrenaline rushing, didn't try to stop it. Her fingers dug into Karl's shoulder and he let out a little mew of pain. She scarcely heard it, but her grip loosened almost instinctively. She tried to hustle him into the lift, but the catmen drifted like leaves in the wind to block their way.

The gold-furred one drew back his lips and hissed. His tail lashed.

Shelly stopped, tried to brazen it out. But she already knew what game they played, knew how they'd try to scratch her up for sport, knew the pain they could cause. Cal had liked to scratch, too, and she still had the scars on her breasts and back to prove it.

They studied her. She studied them, too, her back muscles aching from the tautness of her stance. She shifted. Again the black laughed.

"What the hell do you think you're doing?" Shelly said. Her words had a dangerous edge. Again her grip on Karl's shoulder tightened. "You know them, Karl? Friends of yours? Tell them to take a walk."

"No," Karl whispered. She could barely hear him. "They wouldn't listen. They think it's just play, just fun. Gametime's rare enough. They see I'm out of it, so they won't bother me, but you're someone new and you look fair sport."

"Shit."

"Don't worry. They won't do more than scratch. It's not deathplay."

"Get to the lift," she said, hard, shoving her bag and Johnny's suitcase into Karl's arms and pushing him. He stumbled between the catmen and into the empty car, then blocked the doors open so she could follow.

The gold catman moved to the left. Shelly could see a

little slip of pink tongue showing between his delicate white teeth.

"I don't want to play," she said loudly. "Just let me go and nobody'll get hurt. Fair enough?"

The catman on her right bounded in and out, a blur of black. Shelly felt only a little tug on her pants. When she glanced down, she found a two-inch rip in her daysuit, just below the right knee. Slowly a blood stain grew.

The gold catman crouched for a second. Then he sidled back and forth like a caged animal, his slitted eyes catching the light and shining like emeralds.

"I can play just as rough as you can," Shelly said evenly, fighting the urge to turn and run. They wanted to see her fear, she realized. Probably junked on the smell of adrenaline and sweat. The high of the chase, the kill, *that* called them. They'd gone beyond reason. She forced herself to slow down, to make herself match their movements one for one. That would be her only chance.

A half-purr, half-growl from the black. He moved in fast, then danced away. *Playing with me,* she thought, *taunting, daring.*

Taking a quick step back, she drew her pistol smoothly with her one good hand. Before she could aim, though, the gold catman leaped. He was on her in a millisecond, front claws slashing, hind legs slashing, and she let his momentum carry her back into a roll. Her feet caught him in the stomach and kicked up and over, hard and sharp. She heard a huff of air and a satisfying *crack* as ribs splintered, then the catman sailed over her head, his arms spread wide as if in greeting.

He landed flat on his back, uncatlike for the first time, and moaned softly.

Shelly rolled to the side, half-crouched, the pistol still in her left hand. The black catman paused and tried to stare her down. Only his tail whipped from side to side. Shelly refused to move an inch.

At last the catman bounded over to his friend, reared back, and seemed to become more human than animal once more. He squatted unceremoniously, untabbed the other man's fur skintights, and pulled them open from neck to groin, revealing hairless, web-scarred pink skin. Just below eight small, dark nipples Shelly saw a spreading blue-black discoloration.

She backed into the lift, keeping her pistol ready. Just as the doors started to close the black catman turned and looked at her. His eyes were green-gold and bright as polished steel, unblinking. He was memorizing her face, she knew then, and she had the uncomfortable feeling that she hadn't seen the last of him and his friend.

Then the doors sealed and the lift started down.

The fate of the world's divers societies lies rooted in entropy. All great empires run down. Just as Athens perished at the hands of its primitive Roman students, just as Rome perished at the hands of German barbarians, so shall the United States perish at the hands of its enemies without. I call upon you to help forestall this entropy, to help forestall the destruction of our once-great country. Rise up, ye masses, and we shall make the world new again!

—Joseph S.L. Gilford
An American Voice

—5—

THEY went out a one-way ground-level exit, into the bedlam of centerSprawl. Here haze hung thick in the air, blurring the street, dulling the lights, muting the sounds of the city. The sharp stink of chemicals and open sewage and carbon dioxide and human/animal sweat filled Shelly with a sense of homecoming, of familiarity. She had been born in a section of the city not much different from this one, spent the first eight years of her life there, until her parents had moved to the burbs. Even the buildings looked the same: black slabs of concrete and steel rising all around, the upper floors lost in the gray of haze. And people like a sudden flood of water: punks and straights, skinheads and hackmen, curbside hucksters with everything imaginable, and children wandering in search of any killjoy, and feral animals scavenging the gutters, and old women sitting in doorways muttering to themselves while burning incense on little laptrays—

Karl began coughing. The noise drew Shelly back. "You okay?" she said.

"Yeah," he said, but she could see little flecks of blood at the corners of his mouth. He wasn't in good shape, had to be feeling pain like little knives in his chest with every breath. She didn't like seeing him that way.

"Come on," she said, letting him lean on her shoulders once more. His body felt too hot, feverish; she staggered a bit under the weight but managed to keep walking steadily.

St. Jude Street suddenly loomed before them. It looked far worse than she remembered: a narrow, garbage-strewn alleyway with neon signs blinking and flickering all along its length. And at its mouth sat a sleazy skyeye bar. A few wrought-iron tables and chairs had been set up, and bleary-eyed men and women lounged there breathing oxygen-heavy mixes through masks shaped into beautiful, almost cherubic faces.

At the bar's periphery crouched or sprawled more oxydicts. These watched the breathermasks and the passersby with equal interest, waiting, Shelly guessed, for money for their next fix. Several of them stood unsteadily as she approached with Karl.

One man, gaunt and hollow-eyed, scraggly bearded, bolder than the rest, shoved his way forward. He palmed a six-bladed throwing star with all the subtlety of a Luddite in a computer room.

Shelly swallowed and found her throat suddenly dry. She fought back her impulse to run, knew she'd never get Karl to cover in time. Forcing an expression of calm, she walked straight down the center of the alley, pretending not to notice the throwing star, pretending not to notice the oxydicts or their bar.

She felt the crowd's attention come to a focus and something in her stomach shifted uneasily. Everyone seemed to be looking at her.

She shifted Karl's weight, suddenly, loosening her shoulder-holstered gun in the process. The butt swung close to her fingertips now.

The oxydict stepped forward for his throw, grinning madly, smelling the kill.

Time seemed to stretch too long. As the man pulled back his arm, Shelly drew her gun and fired it in one quick movement. The sharp noise of the shot echoed through the alley. Someone screamed.

The bullet hit the gaunt man in the shoulder, spinning him around and sending him crashing into the wall. He dropped his throwing star and it clattered on the ground like a broken Christmas ornament. Pawing at his wound, he whimpered like a hurt dog.

Nobody moved to help him.

Shelly didn't miss a step. Her tongue felt like dry cotton and her head throbbed. She felt the sweat trickling down her sides and back, felt her heart pounding, felt her fingers cramping from gripping the .38 too hard. This wasn't like planting bombs in turbostations or roughing the feet; she didn't think she could ever get used to fighting streeters, not like this. But she forced a calm expression as she re-holstered her pistol.

The remaining oxydicts looked away and tried to pretend she didn't exist. Shivering a bit, she moved among them, weaving between bodies sprawled on the ground. Only their eyes moved, following her.

A single fact made it a hundred times worse: these were the people, the oppressed masses incarnate, that the Disruption had sworn to help. But when she looked at them, she felt more disgust than pity. Did they deserve to be saved? She didn't know. They didn't care.

She tried to remain aloof, tried to appear supremely confident, but still she felt the rising tension within her, the tide of emotions that pulled her in a dozen directions at once. Fear and distaste that made her want to run—ahead, away, anywhere to escape the oxydicts. Shock. Pain. The thought that she'd betrayed them.

For an instant she longed for Harran's arms around her again, his soft voice whispering Gilford's magic words, those words that always swept her up and carried her on, that filled her with excitement and the strength and the courage to struggle forward. Those words that could move her to tears. Those words that could make her love even the streeters. Gilford's words.

Karl groaned a bit and slumped to the right. Shelly almost lost hold of him but managed to keep him on his feet and moving. As she struggled to move down the alley, she thought she heard soft footsteps, as though a dozen people cat-stepped after her.

She took a quick glance back, half-expecting to find the remaining oxydicts following her. But they weren't. She'd left them behind. She couldn't even see the skyeye bar through the haze anymore.

Sighing, she draped Karl's arm around her shoulder more securely and pressed on with him. A minute later he seemed to regain full consciousness again; he tried to walk. She helped him as best she could.

Thirty meters later, the alley opened up into a regular street. They'd entered from the wrong end, Shelly saw, and she cursed softly. They could have avoided the skyeye bar.

Now shining men and women swirled around her, laughing, reeking of hormones and stimtabs. They passed through denser glittercrowds, masses of gilt/silk/day-glo-dressed burbers mingling with streeters, both frequenting the illicit boutiques only available in holes like St. Jude Street. Hucksters called their wares from doorways. Animen glided through the shadows, stalking one another in intricate games. Musicians played for thrown coins. And all around them, high above, far ahead, left and right, neon signs made the haze glow in tiny globes of soft light.

Nobody paid any attention to Shelly or Karl in all the confusion. *Just as well,* Shelly thought. She felt weak and depressed, empty inside. *They'd just try to kill us.*

A little ahead, a sign jutted far out over the street: ANI-MEN-R-US in dazzling pink letters that pranced back and forth. Shelly went down steep stairs to a basement-level entrance. Karl shuddered violently with every step.

A bell jangled when they pushed the door open, and they found themselves in a small, dim room packed full of bubbling glass tanks. Fuzzy shields of light half-hid the contents from view.

Blinking quickly, trying to get used to the diffuse reddish gold light and the thick, humid smell, Shelly sat Karl on the single straight-backed chair. He moaned softly and clutched his side, rocking back and forth, back and forth.

Shelly took a minute to look around. It seemed a typical bodyshop: behind the color-curtains lay glass chemtanks, the liquids inside foaming and frothing around various modified human and animal body parts. The rooms in back would hold the operating equipment.

Finally the proprietor came out: a huge, lumbering old man whose bald head was covered with snake-scaled skin. His small black eyes peered out from beneath a heavy brow; his smile was slick, oily, very professional.

"I know why you have come!" he said before Shelly could speak. "I have just the thing for you, fresh from the sun-drenched beaches of Mexico." He winked. "The latest fashion to sweep the land—armadillo!" He took her arm and gestured dramatically to the left.

One of the color-screens swirled up and away like a stage curtain rising, and from concealed speakers rose a trumpet call and drum roll. A huge glass-fronted tank in the shape of an armadillo rolled out, and through the thick amber liquid inside it Shelly could see various human-enhanced armadillo parts: bolts of skin covered with a light, grayish plating; black eyes floating loose; sharp black claws at the ends of short-fingered hands.

Something touched her arm and Shelly looked down. The fat man's smooth, cool, reptilian arm curled about hers in loop after loop, its grip tightening slightly, a miniature python trying to choke her wrist to death. His five long, thin, green-scaled fingers wiggled like garter snakes.

Shelly withdrew herself from his circling grasp. "A friend recommended you for your discretion, not your selection."

"Ah? Who, pray tell?"

"Cal."

He nodded. "Yes, yes, dear Cal. But we haven't seen him in such a long while, though, have we. Yes?"

"Yeah. He's long gone."

He nodded. "Ah, well, such regrets. I appreciated his tastes. But now I am forgetting my manners! I should introduce myself to you. I am Esteban Grammatica, owner and chief bodyman of ANIMEN-R-US."

Shelly shrugged. "Names aren't important. My friend here got in a fight and he doesn't want sign nor detail getting back to his parents...they monitor his credit accounts. This'll be a straight cash deal."

Grammatica studied Karl's face for a moment, black eyes unblinking, then walked around him slowly. There was a slightly amused expression on his face; perhaps he didn't believe her story? Shelly wondered.

At last the snakeman said: "Must it be human? We're running a special on otter this week. Imagine the sleek lines of a waterproof pelt—"

"Human," Karl said weakly.

"Very well. But it'll cost extra. We don't get much demand for . . . *humanoform*." There was a measure of disgust in his voice.

"I expected that," Shelly said. "I already know what he needs—Flexisteel ribs, remuscled, and a skinjob on the face."

"That it?"

She held up her three-fingered hand. "Two more of these."

Grammatica's arm wrapped around her wrist, pulling her stubs up to his face. His eyes rolled back in their sockets and a new pair of pupils appeared, these smaller and steel-colored. He studied her fingers for a long moment, his breath strangely hot on her skin, and Shelly had the impression he was reading more than the serial numbers off her stubs.

"Korean," he said at last. "Expensive. I don't have anything comparable in stock. I'd have to send out for it."

"How long?"

"Half, maybe three-quarters of an hour."

"Get to it, then."

"First," he said, "there's the matter of payment. For the lot I'll make a blanket offer. Five millions."

Shelly snorted. "A bit greedy, don't you think?"

"Not," he said, "with no questions asked."

"One million, and you're robbing us blind!"

"Citizen!" he said, sounding shocked and hurt. His black eyes rolled down into place, glistening like polished gems. "That would hardly cover the parts alone! Four millions. I could not take a newdollar less."

"Two."

"Three. And payment now."

"Agreed," Shelly said smugly.

The snakeman turned and shouted, "Paul! Get your lazy paws out here! Customers!"

A moment later a large dog trotted out from behind one

of the curtains of shifting light. Paul looked like a German shepherd, except for his human face and five-fingered front paws. His tail wagged a bit hesitantly.

"Woof?" he said, looking from Shelly to Karl and back again.

"Take the man into the back. Start on his Flexisteel ribs. I'll do the face myself."

"Yeah." Tongue lolling out, he looked at Karl. There was a hunger, a bloodlust, in his gaze that Shelly didn't like. "This way."

With a groan, Karl stood. He followed Paul back through the curtain of light. Far off, Shelly heard the dog-man giving Karl instructions.

"Now," Esteban Grammatica said, "three millions."

Shelly opened her Simsung bag and began pulling out bundles of thousands. She set them on the straight-backed chair in little stacks. At last she finished.

"That's not enough," the snakeman said without even counting. He picked up a bundle and flipped through it, stopped for a second and frowned, studied it, then tossed it back on the chair. "And they're phony."

"You'd know where to pass it off."

"Perhaps. But it's more trouble than the stuff's worth. Still, out of the generosity of my heart I might give you fifty to the dollar."

"That's shit. Ninety."

He shrugged, shoulders writhing like twin serpents. "Forget it, then. You will go elsewhere?"

Shelly bit her lip, knowing Grammatica was ripping her —and that she'd have to let him get away with it. "Okay. I gotta spend it. There's eight-hundred kay here. That's four hundred paid."

"Still quite a bit short."

She closed her Simsung bag and picked up Johnny's

suitcase, thumbed back the locks, opened it. "Are you willing to trade?"

Grammatica's black eyes bulged as he stared at the contents of the case. "Too hot for me!" He took a step back. The tip of a thin, pointed tongue flicked across his lips. "I can deal with Disruptionists—yes, I knew that's what you were the moment you walked in—but I never touch hardware. And the stuff you have is cee-pure trouble! Clockers. Snake-eyes. Slamjams, for Chrissake! I want it out of here. *Now!*"

"Who can take it?"

"I don't know. I don't touch the stuff. You might try the black door ten meters down. But if you tell them I sent you, your friend's dogmeat. Literally."

"Yeah," Shelly said, thinking of the hunger in Paul's dog eyes. "I bet." She snapped the case shut and picked it up by the handle. "I'll be back soon with the rest of the cash. Order my fingers."

The snakeman only grinned his oily slick grin.

She went back out into St. Jude Street, turned right, saw a black door set flush to the alley wall. It had to be the one Grammatica meant: security pads had been set in the brick wall to its right. When she stepped up before them and pressed the handpad, they scanned her a dozen different ways.

"What do you want?" The voice—mechanical, sexless —came from a small speaker

"I've got something to sell. If the price is right."

Something buzzed, then the door opened smoothly, revealing a long white corridor with light panels set at regular intervals overhead. She entered. The door closed quietly behind her.

A tall, thin man with a shaved head stepped from an arched doorway to the right. He wore a silver one-piece suit, and black glasses hid his eyes. "This way," he said, turning.

Shelly followed him into a small room. A white rectangular table stood in its middle, surrounded by cushioned chairs. Another man, identical in appearance to the first, already sat there. His perfectly manicured hands were folded before him.

The first man sat beside his companion. "You have something you wish to sell," he said.

"Yes." She sat down, set the suitcase on the table, thumbed it open, and showed the men the neatly packaged contents: the clockers and snake-eyes and slamjams, the brainjack, the rest.

Both men removed their dark glasses and leaned forward. The first had eyes of transparent glass; the second, eyes of shining steel—augmented for work with micromaterials, Shelly knew. Their gazes were harsh, disconcerting, and she shifted uneasily before them.

"These materials are not yours," said the glass-eyed man.

"They are now."

"The previous owner will seek them."

"His bad luck, then. He ditched me when I needed him and left his stuff behind."

Glass-eyes shook his head slowly, once, twice, three times. "I think I do not believe you. I know this equipment. I built much of it."

"So you're a moralist?"

"A friend."

She laughed. "No tech is a friend. You're stalling. Make an offer or I'll find someone who will."

He pursed his lips and looked at the steel-eyed man, who nodded ever so slightly.

"Five million. Cash."

"It's worth ten times that."

"It will be hard to dispose of. The previous owner has many allies who would ask questions. We agree it's worth more; we decline to pay full value because of the nature of this deal."

Shelly swallowed. How much was Johnny's equipment really worth? She didn't know. She watched both men, tried to see behind the masks of their eyes. *Do they have souls?* she wondered. She saw only her own reflection, distorted, bloated.

"Five million," the glass-eyed tech said again.

Since she needed the cash now, she decided to accept the offer. She didn't have time to shop for a better deal.

Just as she started to speak, a hand reached over her shoulder and pushed the suitcase's lid closed. The latch clicked.

"Hello, Shelly," a too-familiar voice said.

If you wound a man, he will revenge himself on you. If you kill him, his relatives will avenge him. If you kill his whole family, his neighbors will pursue you. But they will not chase you very far or very fast, for they are not involved. This same principle must be applied to the overthrow of any government.

—Joseph S.L. Gilford
The Cold Within

—6—

"**H**ello, Johnny," she said, hard. "You bastard." Again she felt the shock of his betrayal. He'd lied to her. He'd used her. And then he'd ditched her in the middle of a fight.

How did he find me? The techs must've called him, she thought. Or had he a beeper hidden somewhere in his bag. It didn't matter now; he was here and he'd caught her unprepared. All her plans for a quick fix-up and escape seemed suddenly, utterly impossible. Now she had to face the consequences of her theft, and she expected a fight. Slowly she shifted, imperceptibly loosening her .38 in its holster.

But Johnny just picked up his suitcase. "Let's go," he said. "We've got to talk.".

He didn't sound the least bit upset, but Shelly'd watched him long enough to know he never showed his true emotions. He could be planning to shoot her outside as soon as she turned her back. Or he could have something worse, something infinitely more painful in mind. It would be more like him to wait until they were alone.

"Stay away from me or I'll kill you," she snarled. "I never make the same mistake twice!" She drew her gun. The techs started, then settled back to watch impassively; this wasn't their fight. They wouldn't help or hinder either Johnny or her, and they'd be only too glad to do business with the survivor.

Johnny's patient smile mocked her. "What happened was necessary, Shel. You know me better than that. Only the Disruption matters, and I've struck such a blow for freedom that the world itself will shake before the month is through. Important things are happening, Shel, things more important than any single person. Or any single person's feelings, and that includes me."

"That's Gilford talking, not you!"

He nodded. "Of course it is. Gilford's right, you know. He's always been right, and he always will be—such is the lot of a messiah. Now we have work to do."

"Do our leaders know?"

He laughed again, harshly, bitterly. "We're solo as of yesterday, no longer with the bureaucrats. We can do more for the Disruption without them. Now, the plan is already unfolding and I need to supervise it . . . and I'll need your help. Come on." Bowing slightly to the two techs, he turned and started for the door.

Very slowly, Shelly stood. She hesitated, her insides all jumbled, her thoughts and emotions running at odds. He didn't seem angry at anything she'd done. He didn't seem concerned at all. Even her threats to kill him hadn't thrown a glitch into his plans, hadn't slowed him for a heartbeat. Face flushed, she reholstered her pistol. Her hands tightened and she felt little pricks of pain in the stubs of her amputated fingers.

"Damn you," she whispered.

Johnny stopped in the doorway, looking back. When she met his gaze, he smiled that jack-dumb smile of his like a lost puppy in need of help. She felt a softening inside, a compassion she longed to deny, but somehow never could. And then her anger slowly drained away, leaving her fears and hurts like so many glittering jewels in her mind, like so many shattered rainbows. He'd used her, yes, but there had to be a purpose. He wasn't a fool. And the Disruption mattered more than any single person; even Karl, even her. Even Johnny Zed.

The least she could do was hear him out, see what his plans were. And if he'd spoken the truth, if he'd really done something to defeat Congress, then she certainly wanted to be there when the deathblow came.

Slowly, keeping her hand near her pistol, she followed him into the corridor. Behind her, the door slid closed with an all too final click.

Johnny didn't say a word on the way to Grammatica's shop. Shelly walked a half step behind and to his left, watching his every move. A bit to her surprise, he put up with her paranoia with almost nauseating calmness. It made her feel infinitely guilty for not trusting him.

"How much money do you have with you?" she finally asked, as they went down the steps to ANIMEN-R-US.

"Enough," he said.

"Two million six?"

"Enough."

When he shoved open the door, Grammatica came scurrying in from the other room, calling, "You have the money, yes?" Then he came up face to face with Johnny and his thin lips tightened. "Again you come here? But you said you were finally satisfied!"

Shelly looked from one to the other. "You've met?"

The snakeman nodded. "I did all his modifications, my very best work. Supremely clever. Supremely complex. And very, very crafty. It hardly shows up on the best monitors, and you'd think the human would be grateful for all the extra effort, yes?"

"You were paid," Johnny said, "and more than the job was worth. Where's Karl?"

"Dog's working him over in the back."

Johnny nodded. "Good. You're not letting him do the face, I trust."

"Certainly not! For such work there is only one who is gifted enough. I am the only *true* metaform artist."

"Of course, of course." Johnny's smile was patronizing. "I will have new specifications for him shortly—they're coming by courier. I trust you can follow nonstandard neural prints?"

"I," said Grammatica, sounding extremely put upon, "am deeply wounded by your insinuations."

"And what's this about a three-million tag on the job?"

"Gotta make a profit." He shrugged. "You know."

"Charge it to Tech House. Usual rates."

Grammatica started to protest, but Johnny waved him down. "You know the deal," he said. "You want them to drop their protection? Seems to me the feet would torch this place within an hour, if word got out . . ."

"No, no," Grammatica said reluctantly. "How you make me suffer! So shall it be, though. I, poor humble shopkeeper that I am, want no trouble from anyone, feet or techs or not. Yes?"

Johnny nodded. "Just do a good job and I'll make sure you get your usual bonus."

Shelly had kept tactfully silent as they talked, but she

couldn't help wondering what they meant. Protection? Special modifications on Johnny? Neural blueprints for Karl's rebuild? She didn't like the sound of any of that, but she had no intention of asking for more details. The less she knew, the healthier she'd stay. She'd realized Johnny was a technical boy the minute they met but hadn't known he hung out with people like the techs and Grammatica. They unnerved her more than she liked to admit. And, if they had their own underground protection network, she certainly didn't want to cross them. She had the distinct impression, suddenly, that the techs she'd talked to in the room had been setting her up, stalling her until Johnny could arrive. She didn't like the feeling.

Still grumbling a bit, Esteban Grammatica coiled his arm around her wrist and pulled her toward the back room, toward the operating rooms. "Your Korean fingers came," he said, "and lucky you, they're the latest upgrade. In fact, since the techs are paying, I'll do both your hands, eight and two. We shall doubletime it. I don't want you, and I don't want *him*"—a jerk of the head toward Johnny—"hanging around here more than necessary. Disruptionists and techs are bad for business, you know. Yes?"

"I can imagine," Shelly said. She wanted out of there rather badly herself.

They pushed through the curtain into a wide hallway with shimmerscreened doors to either side. More animal parts bubbled in closed tanks along the walls, and antiseptic gave the air a sickly sweet smell. The place had been soundeadened, but Shelly could still hear the high-pitched whine of a neuro-enhancer from behind one of the doors. That would be Paul working on Karl, she decided. She felt a sympathetic twinge in her own ribs at the thought of his operation.

"This way, please. Yes?" Grammatica palmed a doorpad

and one of the shimmerscreens dissolved, revealing a room filled with polished stainless-steel equipment, all of it clustered around a chair with wrist clamps on the arms.

The chair looked more like a medieval torture device than anything else, Shelly decided as she settled into it. Grammatica buckled her wrists down and spread her wounded hand on a palmpad so he could get to the fingers. A tray whirled out from the wall, and on it Shelly saw dozens of gleaming surgical tools, little bonesaws, microprobes, a neuromancer.

Grammatica picked up a scalpel and looked at her fingers, smiling, suddenly eager, suddenly absorbed in his work. Horror vids of mad bodyshop owners flashed to Shelly's mind, but she forced them away. Then she remembered the hunger in Paul's dog eyes, and she could not help but wonder if excess human flesh ever made it out the door.

Nodding, Grammatica bent toward her, scalpel poised.

"Don't forget the anesthetic," she said, voice sharp.

He smiled sweetly, fingers winding around the scalpel in coil after coil after coil. "Would I do that?"

Shelly heard a hissing sound, and something sharp and ice cold touched her neck. Then the world got blurry and dropped from sight like the opening frames of an old vid badly translated to 3-D.

When she woke, it was to a pleasantly warm darkness scented with flowers . . . roses, she thought idly. That had to be Johnny's touch: he was ever the romantic. And, perhaps, it might have been a peace offering.

Stretching, she felt her new fingers move with a suppleness and subtlety her old ones hadn't had. Grammatica, whatever his thoughts of her and Johnny Zed, of the Disruption and the techs, had certainly done an excellent job. Her fingers felt stronger, more sensitive, all around *better* than the ones Hanging Charlie'd sold her three years before. Only part of it could be explained by the upgrade; the rest had to be the snakeman's talent with a neuro-enhancer. She knew why Johnny Zed had used Grammatica; Johnny took only the very best.

And where was Johnny? For that matter, where was *she*?

When she sat up, her gaze fell on the opticon controls, and lights in the ceiling corners came on, bright enough to see by but dim enough not to hurt her eyes. She was in a small but elegantly furnished room, she saw, and it didn't have any windows. That alone made her distinctly uneasy. The dresser, the bed with its carved headboard, the table and lamps—they were all made of real wood with matching silver designs etched into them, plush, extravagant. She knew then that this was not a burber's home, and certainly not the sort of place any self-respecting Disruptionist would own. But neither was it the sort of austere chrome-and-glass hitech playground a tech would have. Only one sort of person owned a house with a room like this, and that was a congressman. She swallowed uneasily.

What would Harran do? she wondered. *What would Johnny Zed do?* Wait, she decided, wait and see what developed. There had to be a reason for her being here, and as soon as she found out what it was, only *then* would she act.

Standing, she shucked her nightgown and methodically checked her body for unwarranted tampering that Grammatica or anyone else might have done while she was unconscious. Everything seemed in place, and as she flexed her new fingers, she decided she was in excellent working order.

She searched the dresser and found plenty of clothing, all in her size. Her host had certainly done an exceptionally good job of preparing for her. Unfortunately, most of the clothes tended toward decadently ornate gowns, expensive designer suits, and other things not at all to her tastes. The wardrobe had to have cost a small fortune, enough to finance their cell for quite a few years. Shelly shook her head as she thought of the waste. Finally, though, she picked out a plain black daysuit and put it on, followed by good black boots.

After sealing the waist tabs, she realized she'd lost quite a bit of weight: the suit was baggier than it should have been, made her look like she'd been starving for a month. How long had she been unconscious? Long enough for her fingers to heal, she thought. Long enough for her to lose fifteen pounds. That meant at least a week, probably two.

The door opened easily to her touch. As she peered up and down the white-carpeted corridor, she noted the oil paintings on the walls, the chairs richly upholstered in red velvet, the intricately carved realwood furniture. Like her room, the corridor had no windows; light came from intricate cut-glass chandeliers overhead. Noticing a tiny vidcamera hidden in one of the chandeliers, she just sighed.

Well, whoever had brought her here obviously knew she was awake. It set her at an almost complete disadvantage anyway, so she stepped out in the open. After all, she thought, if her host had wanted her dead, he could easily have murdered her in her sleep.

A small, dark man in an outrageously outdated tuxedo appeared at the far end of the corridor. His mustache had been waxed at the tips and his hair combed back. He bowed ever so slightly.

"This way, please, Miss Tracer," he said. He had a vaguely British accent.

Shelly didn't move. "Who are you?" she demanded. "And where am I?"

"I am Jeeves, madam, the butler. If you would please accompany me, you will find Mr. Zed and Senator Winston waiting in the drawing room. I am sure they wish to explain everything to you themselves."

Johnny with a senator? That didn't sound good. But if he was there, she knew he'd have a good reason. Perhaps, she thought, this would be their first solo assignment: an assassination. She smiled a bit. Yes, that made sense—a true blow for freedom, more than the Disruption had ever managed to do! "Very well," she said to Jeeves. "Take me to them."

Turning, he led her through labyrinthine corridors, all carpeted in white, all with plush chairs and couches in red velvet, all with crystal chandeliers overhead, all fairly reeking of wealth and good taste. It sickened her to think of how the senator had gotten his money—wrung from the innocent workers, no doubt. Yes, she realized, she would enjoy seeing him die, seeing the pain and suffering he had caused round on him and devour him in the end. All Johnny Zed had to do was give the word and she'd try out these new fingers on Senator Winston's fat, bloated neck.

At last Jeeves stopped before a pair of huge wooden doors, doors that would have been more appropriate for a castle than a private home. He rapped twice, waited a heartbeat, then pushed them open.

Shelly couldn't help but notice how they glided on little tracks set in the floor. There had to be more here than just wood. Durasteel cores? It certainly fit in with the lack of windows. They were probably underground, in some sort of blast shelter. It would be just like someone with so much stolen power and wealth to hole up like a packrat, enjoying his treasures with a private little greed.

"Miss Tracer," Jeeves announced with stiff-backed formality.

Shelly shoved past him to look around the huge room in awe. The high-domed ceiling held a sparkling cut-glass chandelier. A marble fountain bubbled in one corner, amid a carefully cultivated Japanese garden complete with bonsai trees. The sweet smell of flowers weighted the air. In the other corners were statues, intricate sculptures, *pièces d'art* that she knew had to be genuine and worth several fortunes: no one would decorate a house like this with anything other than originals.

It took a moment for her attention to focus on the small cluster of couches and chairs in the center of the room. Johnny Zed, she saw, sprawled there in a huge armchair. He wore a simple gray suit and tie, clothing at odds with the richness of his surroundings. He nodded to her with a cheerful grin. And next to him on the sofa—

It was Karl's father. Despite the tailored glitter-gold business suit, she knew him. She felt her heart skip a beat, her stomach twist. He couldn't fail to recognize her, she thought, certain of it, certain that he would call the feet and she and Johnny would be caught or killed. What had Johnny gotten her into? For a second she froze, trying not to look too shocked or horrified, trying to calm her rough breathing. How could she get herself out of his mess?

She recovered enough to crank on a smile.

"Hello, Sandy," she said in a low voice. "I'm pleased to see you again."

A showman once said you can fool some of the people all of the time, or all of the people some of the time, but never all of the people all of the time. Of course he was wrong. All you need is sufficient technology and you can make anybody believe anything, make everybody believe everything.

—Joseph S.L. Gilford
The Waiting Room

—7—

JOHNNY Zed laughed. "Leave us," he said to Senator Winston, who just nodded wearily and headed for the other room.

Shelly watched Sandy's back until the door shut behind him. Then she glared at Johnny. "Have you gone mad?" she demanded. "When did you start ordering senators around?"

"And when did they start obeying?" Johnny asked.

"Damn it, what's going on?"

"That was Karl."

"Bullshit!"

"Truth." He stepped close, took her elbow, guided her to the couch. She found her legs suddenly weak, and there was a sick, fluttery feeling in her stomach. She sat mechanically, and he sat beside her, his arm around her shoulders, pulling her to him. His nearness was warm, comforting. She tried to resist him, tried to keep herself distanced from his overwhelming presence, his overwhelming personality.

"Grammatica—"

"Is the best there is. Just like I am. Just like you are."

"Hah."

"It pays to work with the best. Shelly, you gave me the diversion I needed to make it into the house—and, once inside, it was a simple matter to kidnap Senator Winston and his wife."

"Where are they?"

"Safely out of the way. Unharmed, if that's what you're worried about."

She snorted. "You should have killed them!"

"Bloodthirsty, aren't we today?"

"Fuck you, too, Johnny. I went under for a couple of new fingers, and then I wake up *here*, wherever here is, and find I've been drugged for days. Then it turns out one of my friends has been remade to resemble a senator, and that you've been off kidnapping important people, and now God knows what plans you have for me! Man, the feet and SecurNet are going to be tearing up the Sprawl searching for us! *Why the screaming goddamn fuck did you leave me drugged for so long?*"

In quiet, measured tones he said, "Where do you think we are, Shel?"

That stopped her for a second. "What the hell sort of question is *that*?"

"I'll tell you, then. You're in Senator Winston's D.C. house. You've been here for ten days. For seven of those ten days Karl has been passing socially for the senator."

Shelly swallowed at the lump in her throat. "You're telling the truth, aren't you?"

"Always, Shel."

"God! You'll never get away with it!"

"Sure we will. Karl's blood type is nearly identical to his father's. They have the same build, and now the same features right down to the birthmark on the senator's thigh. *And* Karl knows his father intimately—knows his idiosyncrasies, his mannerisms, his little day-by-day habits. We've fooled everyone so far, right down to the hired help."

"You said you'd struck such a blow for freedom that the world would shake within a month."

He smiled. "Senator Winston is an important man and, better yet, one whose power and influence are still growing. With our help, Karl will establish and expand that power base. We'll use it to undermine Congress's power, make the way clear for the coming revolution."

"That was never Gilford's plan."

He looked at her with those infinitely deep, infinitely old eyes. Softly he smiled. "I know Gilford better than you think, Shel. Anything that will help restore the democracy would please him."

She pushed him away, stood, turned toward the little Japanese garden. The waterfall tinkled faintly, sounding like little bells; she could smell the spray on the faintly stirring air. Again there was confusion in her, the jumble of conflicting thoughts and impulses that pulled her first one way, then another, then back again. Why did Johnny do this to her?

Her voice was hoarse with anger, with hurt, when she spoke again. "Why didn't you wake me, Johnny? Didn't you trust me to keep to the plan?"

"I trust you with my life. If I didn't, you'd be long dead by now."

He said it in such a matter-of-fact tone that she could not help but believe it. Looking back at him, she wondered for the thousandth time what sort of man he was to use her this way, what sort of man he was to expect her to follow him after all he'd done.

"Why ten days?" she whispered.

"You needed to heal."

"And Karl didn't?"

"His face was plasticked and he was in a lot of pain. I didn't envy him his role. But if we're to succeed it had to be done, and he knew it, and he did his part without protest."

She snorted. "I suppose that's an example for me to follow."

"If you wish. But I believe in people making their own choices, and it was easiest for me to put off yours until you were completely healed. Until now."

"Damn you!"

He rose, pulled her to him. "The word," he said, "is Freedom." His body was warm against hers, musked with spicy cologne.

Again Shelly felt the power of his presence, the air of supreme confidence he exuded. It was part of what attracted her to him, and try as she might, she could not deny it. *Pheromones*, she thought for a second. *He's putting them out stronger than anyone I've ever seen*. Perhaps Grammatica was responsible. Perhaps . . .

"It's time to make your choice," he said. "There are three options. I'd like you to join me and Karl and those few who support us. We could use you, your practical mind, your talents."

"Or?"

"Go back to the Disruption and probably get splattered. Or drop out entirely. We can get you a new identity, credit enough to start over. We'll have to mindwipe your last few years, though. This means more to us than anything else, and we couldn't take the chance of your getting picked up by the feet, of them sweating the truth out of you."

She shivered, suddenly cold. The idea of waking up one morning and finding half her life gone was more terrifying than all the battles she'd been through. No, she could never agree to that. And the feet . . . they still had her blood. If she were alone, without an organization to back and cover for her, the feet would stand a much better chance of tracking her.

Johnny simply said, "Will you trust me?"

His voice held strength, authority, the almost electric will to succeed that had always swept her up before. And she wanted to share that power more than anything in the world, wanted to turn it to the purposes of the Disruption. Johnny would succeed. Johnny's plan would succeed. It *had* to. There was no alternative.

"Will you trust me?" he said again.

She looked at his eyes, those jack-dumb lost puppy eyes of his, and she could not deny him. *The word is Freedom.*

"Yes," she said distantly.

"Will you follow me?"

"Yes!"

He paused a heartbeat. "Will you love me?"

She could not help herself. She whispered, "Yes."

He kissed her, and she found herself responding. Her choice was made and she knew she'd follow through to the end. She couldn't ditch him now. To death or victory she would go, and there would be no more doubts, no more looking back. She trusted Johnny Zed with her life. He was all that mattered in the world, for through him the Disruption would succeed. Though the rest of the world didn't know it, he was the last, best hope for Gilford and all those who hated Congress. She was as certain of that as she'd ever been of anything in her life.

They made love on the couch by the fountain, the scent of flowers thick around them, and when they were done Shelly looked at Johnny Zed's peaceful, calm face. He reminded her of Harran, of all they'd had together . . . no, not Harran, she decided at last. He reminded her of Gilford. At his prime Gilford must have been like Johnny, burning with the passions of life, burning with the power of his beliefs. Thus had the Disruption been born.

Johnny was better though, bright and hot as a new flame, burning with power and charisma. She knew he would not fail. He was the best there was.

The French had a saying—noblesse oblige—to describe the duties of the ruling class. However, the British were the only ones to understand the concept, to understand the responsibilities that come with power and position. That is why the King of England is still alive. If the ruling class fails in its duty to society—as it did in France, and Russia, and China— is it any surprise that the people rise up to set things aright once more? Here, in America, Congress has forgotten its duty. I leave the conclusion to you.

—Joseph S.L. Gilford
The Enemy Without

—8—

"**T**HEY'LL kill us," Shelly said, trying to keep her voice from breaking. "They'll know who we are. Security will have us flat on the ground before you can spit!"

The last half-hour had been one mad scramble after another: Karl's father had been invited to a private party at Lymington Bartholomew Jones's palatial home—Jones being the Speaker of the House—but Karl and Johnny had failed to note the invitation until the appointed hour was nearly upon them. Since not showing up for the party would have been a faux pas that would not have passed unnoticed in many of the correct social circles; and since Jones was a Very Important Person in congressional politics, and they wanted his support when Karl made his bid for power, Johnny had decided Karl-as-Senator had to attend.

Now Johnny just laughed. "Get calm," he said, "slicker down. We're listed as the senator's aides on every Secur-Net from here to Asia. I made the entries myself. We'll check out right on anything a mere congressman can come up with."

"A mere congressman? There's no such thing!"

Karl looked at her. "It isn't like you to panic. If Johnny says it's okay, it's okay. Right?"

Curtly, she forced a nod. "I guess."

Johnny said, "Nobody will look twice. I'd stake my life on it." Then he grinned and winked.

You've staked all our lives on it, Shelly thought. *This better not be your first mistake.*

As the aircar nosed toward the ground, she forced herself into the routine of checking her personal armaments. She tightened the strap of her shoulder holster, then straightened her dinner jacket and ran the tabs shut again so the bulge of her pistol hardly showed. Quickly she ran a mental inventory of the weapons she carried: the spring-knives attached to her wrists, the razor-sharp fingernails of her left hand, the stun grenades in her belt's secret compartment. Damn but she wished Johnny'd let her take her Simsung bag! She felt almost naked without her plastic explosives and other, more lethal, devices close at hand.

When she'd asked for them, Johnny'd merely said: "Now isn't the proper time for those. We're going as the senator's aides, remember, and that means you're not allowed to *kill* anyone!"

And, she thought, Johnny's plan or no, it would have been a terrible temptation for her to try to murder some (if not most) of the people present at Representative Jones's party. Her jaw tightened as she thought of how close she'd be to some of the people on the Disruption's prime-target list.

With a sigh, she turned and gazed out the aircar's window at the vast darkened land flowing like an ocean below. Here the trees and hedges became little reefs thrusting above the waves of lawn; here the flower gardens became great rolling breakers, their white blossoms spray against the deeper colors of grass and mulch; here the goldfish ponds and boating lakes glistened with starlight and became, for an instant, small islands set like diamond studs along their path. The grounds were beautiful. The grounds were empty. It seemed an immense waste; without people to use and enjoy the estate, it could never be more than a frivolous pleasure, a private thing to be hoarded and secretly enjoyed. It was a sign of the decadence all around her. Still, Shelly knew she should've expected such horrors; D.C. was the Senate's playground, after all, and you needed megamoney to live here. Jones, as Speaker of the House, certainly had that.

"I still can't believe we're doing this," she said. "What if someone from the Disruption recognizes us?"

Karl touched her arm lightly: his hand, she noticed, trembled almost constantly now. "No one will recognize me," he said distinctly, "and if someone spots you or Johnny, they'll have some explaining to do . . . and I'll be on the Committee of Examinations looking into their association with the Disruption. You've got to adjust your perspective, Shel. This isn't nickel-and-dime terrorism anymore. This is all-out subversion, and we've got to play, and win, by turning Congress's own rules against it."

"Exactly," Johnny said, grinning.

"That's—" She almost said "Gilford speaking," but it wasn't. It was Johnny Zed. She bit her lip and looked out the window, away from them.

"We can win," Karl said again. "We *can*. But we won't if we show the slightest weakness."

Something about him disturbed her, something more than the changes in his appearance. As she thought about him, she decided it was the hardness he'd taken on. Before, in the Disruption, she'd judged him the weakest link in her cell. Now their roles seemed reversed, him so quiet and calm and competent with his senator role, she as nervous and jittery as the rawest of recruits. That realization alone was enough to make her distinctly uneasy. And, to top it all, Johnny was sitting back in his seat, watching her through slitted eyes, a faint smile on his lips. He was enjoying it. Putting people off their guard had always been one of his strong points. *But still . . .*

Finally she sighed. "If you say it'll work, I believe you."

Johnny inclined his head ever so slightly.

Shelly looked out the aircar's window again. A yellow glow lit up the sky ahead, and as the aircar cleared one final reef of trees, she saw Jones's floodlit house. It was a sprawling, Victorian monstrosity, three stories high with intricate gingerbreading around the doors and windows and more than a fair number of chimneys. Long white tables had been set up outside, on the neatly manicured lawn, and dozens if not hundreds of glitterdressed men and women wandered about.

Shelly could hear their driver's voice, distant, muted through the bulkhead, as he talked to the estate's SecurNet link. Everything seemed to check, so, repellers whirring, they descended further, touching down near the other transports on the private landing pad to the far side of the building.

Their aircar's door hissed open. Johnny put on an ambivalent expression and trotted down the steps two at a time, jaunty in his stride, for a quick looksee at the people coming to meet them. He seemed to approve; he called back, "Your show, Senator."

Sighing, Karl stood and stretched. Then he smiled a plastic smile and walked out, head high, shoulders rigidly back. His movements were slow and studied, the movements of an old man experienced with the world. But then, Shelly thought, he didn't have to walk or talk quickly anymore; he was important enough for the world to wait for him.

It was a hand-shaking, back-slapping, everyone-knows-everyone sort of party, with the glitterdressed people wandering from one to another to babble on with their shallow talk. They eddied and swirled around Karl, their robes brilliant gold or silver, a few more reserved in gray or white nightsuits, all of them asking questions at once, gathering opinions, hanging to his every word. *Shallow. Glitterdressed.* Like moths drawn to a flame, they rushed to him and to the other men and women of import, and Shelly, unknown by and unknowing of them, found herself shouldered aside, unheeded.

She drew herself back to a darker part of the yard to keep a more covert watch. It looked like a long, dull evening lying for her; luckily she still had her duties to perform. Should anyone try to assassinate Karl, unlikely though it was *here*, she'd be ready to splatter him good.

For a time she amused herself by drawing mental targets on the few people she recognized from the NewsNets. A needlegun would be best, she decided, taking imaginary aim at Doloria Voltaire, a representative whose landgrabbing had thrown fifty thousand people out of a low-rent downSprawl district not three months before. One quick shot, and a tiny steel needle could pierce her eye and enter her brain. Then, five seconds later, a small explosion . . .

"Good evening," said a low voice to her left.

Startled, she turned and found a man standing beside her. He was tall and thin, with ash-blond hair just turning to gray, sharp features, a lightly cleft chin. His eyes were darker than any she'd ever seen before, and when he smiled his teeth were perfect and white. No man, she thought, could look so perfect naturally.

"Hello," she said uneasily.

"You came with the senator?"

She nodded. "I'm one of his aides. . . . He insisted I come, though he doesn't seem to need me."

The man shook his head. "He's in rare form tonight; I haven't seen him so active in ten years. But then, he doesn't get to many parties anymore, and especially not without his wife. She's not ill, I trust."

"No, no." She laughed. Johnny had schooled her on what to say when asked about Julia Winston. But then, Johnny had schooled her on everything, from the shallowest of party talk to the most probing of questions. "They had a tiff and Ms. Winston left for an extended vacation abroad. I expect she'll be back before the month's out, when her credit's used up."

"No doubt. Ah, but I'm forgetting my manners. I'm Lee Jones."

Shelly felt an almost electric shock go through her. "The Speaker of the House?"

"The same. And you?"

"Shelly Tracer, sir."

He sighed. "Such formality! Call me Lee, please. Everyone does."

"Of course, Lee." She could smell his musk now, spicy, alternately hot and sweet. It was making her slightly dizzy. All the horrors Jones was said to have perpetrated, all the assassinations he'd ordered, all the crimes that had been committed in his name . . . She felt her new fingers itch at the thought of shooting him. Slowly she forced her hands to her sides, away from her gun, and painfully she smiled for him. She was doing this for Karl and Johnny, she reminded herself. For them and the good of the Disruption she would let him live.

He smiled again, saying, "Have you had anything to eat?"

"Not yet."

"Then I insist you try the pâté. Something new from the colonies, you know." Grinning infectiously, he offered her his arm.

A bit to her surprise, Shelly found herself taking it. Jones's charm was immense; he certainly wasn't the monster she'd expected. From the Disruption's reports on him, she'd expected more of a hulking ogre, rather than a polished, eloquent gentleman. It wasn't hard to like him. Still, she had to remind herself, he was her enemy, her sworn foe. It was because of people like him that she'd joined the Disruption in the first place. Mentally she constructed a brick wall, putting herself on one side, him on the other.

Laughing gently, he led her into the crowd. Colors swirled around them, scents of stimtabs and exotic drugs, alcohol and flashbase. "This is Ginna, and Sal, and David," he said as they passed glitterdressed people. They all nodded to her, to Lee, with half-vacant smiles.

The tables held all sorts of delicacies, Shelly found: imported meats and cheeses, exotic wines, stimtabs in little silver boxes, enough food and drugs to keep a district sated for a week. He helped her fill her plate with all manner of things she didn't recognize.

"I'm not sure I can eat all this!" she laughed, when he began stacking melon balls into little pyramids.

"The secret of all good food," he whispered in a mock-serious voice, "is to make anything as insubstantial as possible. That way people can eat all they want and not feel guilty about it later."

"I see." She smiled back and felt the bricks in her mind dissolving one by one. She might learn to enjoy herself here, she thought. Could the Disruption have been wrong about him? He was certainly not the monster she'd been led to expect.

"I've got more friends for you to meet," he said. He took her elbow and steered her back into the crowd.

As she nibbled a cracker spread with something she couldn't quite identify, Lee introduced her to a dozen more people. They were more a blur of faces than anything else, but she had the impression they were somehow associated with Congress . . . some aides, some advisers, a few youths due to inherit a family seat many years hence—

As they walked, Lee told her jokes and funny stories of congressional mishaps. Shelly found herself getting swept up in the power of his words, surrounded, enthralled. He had a presence not unlike Johnny's or Harran's, she decided: he was accustomed to power and knew how to wield it.

Finally she noticed the crowds were eroding away; a slow but steady migration toward the aircars had begun. When she looked at her watch, she discovered it was nearly three in the morning, much later than she'd thought.

Lee had noticed, too. He sighed. "I guess it's time for you to leave, too?"

She nodded. "It's late."

"Come again tomorrow night, love," he said. "I'm having a quiet reception for some of my closest friends. I'd very much like to see you again. Come?"

"I . . . I don't know. It depends on the senator, you see, whether he's got any work for me to do. You understand?"

He laughed. "Sandy's all work, love. If it would help, I can have a chat with him, perhaps pry you out of his clutches . . . ?"

"I'd rather you didn't. It might upset him. He gets a bit protective."

"I understand. Until tomorrow, then, if you can make it." He gave a brief bow. "Adieu. And if not tomorrow, then certainly another time." He kissed her lightly on the cheek, then brushed past her.

More slowly now, her face and body tingling, Shelly wandered back to where Johnny and Karl were talking quietly. Most of the glitterfolk had disappeared; almost everyone had gone. Already maids and servants moved through the grounds, cleaning up, putting things right once more.

"I see you found a friend," Johnny said. There was a touch of disapproval in his tone.

Shelly bristled at that. "What would you have me do, snub the host? Smart, that. Get us kicked out."

"Just watch him. He's dangerous."

"He seemed quite . . . well, *nice*. Not at all what I expected. He invited me to a party tomorrow night."

"Don't go," Karl said. "He's not so kind as he seems."

Johnny laughed and shook his head. "No," he said. "I want you to go. The whole idea is marvelous! Watch sharp and there's no telling what you'll learn. Karl and I have enough work to keep us occupied. Besides, you might enjoy yourself."

"I'll think about it," Shelly said. She hated decisions like this one, where duty and friendship tore at her from so many different sides at once. "I'll let you know tomorrow."

Karl just shook his head disapprovingly. "I know you, Shel. You'll go. And you'll regret it."

At that, she had to laugh.

There is more to life than life itself. There are values, emotions ...intangible things which transcend physical well-being. If man is to survive, he must be more than mere organisms scattered across a planet; he must be a collective operating as a unit, working for the well-being of all. This is how I defend revolution against tyranny.

—John Zedowski
Collected Essays

—9—

THE next evening Shelly went to Lee Jones's house. Since it was a private party, and since Karl hadn't been invited, Johnny thought it best that she drive herself there.

Again she glided over the estate's rolling grounds, and as she did her thoughts of all the wasted effort and money returned. Such extravagance ought to infuriate her, she thought, and it did in a coldly academic way. But it was hard to hate the Speaker of the House, hard to keep herself remote and withdrawn from a person who'd become more than a name and vid image to her. She was here, she reminded herself, as a spy, not an ally; she had to keep that in mind at all times.

When she landed, a black man dressed in a white suit came to greet her. "Good evening," he said with the faintest trace of a New England accent. "You must be Miss Tracer. Mr. Jones is expecting you."

"Thank you."

"This way, please."

At first she'd taken him for a servant, but then she noticed the bulge of a gun beneath his suit coat, and there was something odd about the pupils of his eyes. He had to be a metaman, she decided, probably from SecurNet, whose job it was to guard all government officials.

She followed him into a large, ornately furnished hallway, past open doors revealing tantalizing glimpses of elegantly furnished rooms. One thing was certain: Jones had excellent taste. Either that or with his money he could afford to buy it.

At last the man in white pulled back a pair of doors. A haze of green smoke drifted out, and through it Shelly could see the reclined forms of various people she'd met at the party the night before. This had to be Jones's circle of friends and followers, she decided. More glitterfolk, though they were plainly dressed tonight.

As she moved forward the green smoke surrounded her, penetrated her skin and made her tingle all over. She recognized it at once: Narcodrone, a neurostimulant she'd tried once or twice in school. It was expensive, a vice only the wealthy could regularly indulge in, or indulge in to such an extent.

Lee saw her and rose from a mat on the other side of the room, calling a welcome. "I'm glad you escaped!" he said. "The senator's work must be rather dull for someone like you."

She smiled. "Not at all. He gave me the night off, since he had a lot of reading to catch up on."

Lee chuckled. "If he'd bother to have optical scanners and data feeds put into his eyes . . ."

"He's still a bit old-fashioned, I'm afraid. But that's also why he hired me—I'm a bit closer to the cutting edge of technology than he is."

"Oh?" Lee's eyebrows rose. "What's your specialty, dear?"

"Antiterrorism."

"Interesting. I never would have guessed."

Shelly eased into a smile. "It's purely theoretical, I assure you. I don't think I'd stand up a day in the field against the Disruptionists."

"You might surprise yourself."

"I hope never to have the chance to find out." She forced a shudder. "It's better to keep them out than to try to kill them."

"Why don't you sit beside me, so we can talk some more." He escorted her to a group of flowseats and sprawled in one. Shelly took the one to his right, leaned back and smiled as it analyzed her bone structure and began a deep, soothing massage. That, with the drugs in the air, made her sleepy, drawn out. She didn't quite relax —there were too many fears and inhibitions fighting within her—but she did settle back and let herself drift.

"May I ask," Lee said, "how long you intend to stay with the senator? Antiterrorism is a field I'm interested in myself, and I'm sure I'd be able to put you to better use in my organization. The Disruption seems to have made me one of their prime targets, and I'm often being inconvenienced by their little pranks."

"But you don't even know my qualifications!" Shelly said. "How can you be sure I'd fit in?"

He laughed. "The senator has a reputation for being most thorough in his investigations. If you're working for him, you've passed a better background sweep than even I could provide. And the senator only hires the best. It's as simple as that. As for whether you'd fit in, well, I have a feeling about you, love. I think you're good, very good, in your field. You have a quiet, hard way about you which I find fascinating."

Shelly tried to laugh it away. "I think you're flattering me!"

"Of course." He took her hand. His eyes were dark, so dark, Shelly thought, and mysterious. "How about it? Work for me? You don't have to leave the senator; perhaps a bit of freelancing on the side, duplicating his security measures?"

"I'll have to think about it," Shelly said, and she smiled as smoothly as Johnny or Harran ever did. "I'll let you know."

After that, conversation turned to more petty things. The atmosphere changed; new drugmists hissed in from the corners of the room.

Shelly found herself laughing, talking, playing simple childhood games such as tag and hide-and-seek with the other glitterfolk. They seemed to accept her, to welcome her among them, and for the first time in many years she actually felt she belonged in their company.

The rest of the evening was a blur. Shelly had vague memories of driving home very late, of stumbling into her room and collapsing in bed.

When she woke, the sun was already high. The light from the window hurt her eyes and she groaned, turning her head away. She was painfully aware of all the indulgences she'd been through the night before. Her skin felt cold and numb from the Narcodrone she'd breathed, and her head pounded from the alcohol, and her lungs burned ever so faintly from stimtabs. She wasn't accustomed to the glitterfolk and their diversions; she felt dirty, used. She was reminded of the morning following the first time she'd lost her virginity.

There was a knock on her door, then Johnny stuck his head in. "Ready to go?"

She groaned. "Where?"

"Don't you remember? I'm certain I sent you a memo. There's a special joint congressional meeting scheduled for this afternoon, and we both have to be there with the senator."

Sitting up, she looked blearily at him. "I guess I forgot."

"Well, get dressed, and remember: no personal weapons this time."

"Right."

He laughed. "You're a mess, Shel. I'll get you something for your crash."

She didn't deign to reply, her head hurt so much.

They left in less than an hour. Karl's private aircar picked them up, then bore them away.

Shelly stayed by the window most of the way, looking down on the rolling grasslands of D.C., observing with great interest the huge monuments to Congress... Monticello, the Congressional Monument, the White House, the Statue of Liberty.

By the time they reached the immense, five-sided congressional complex, Shelly was feeling much better. Johnny had grown strangely quiet, though, and looked more than a bit depressed. He obviously hated dealing with senators and congressmen, she decided.

To cheer him up, she said, "Don't you want to hear about last night?"

"Hmm?" He looked at her, his smile broadening. "Of course, Shel. What happened?"

Karl leaned forward, too. "Yes. Was he as pleasant in private as you thought he'd be?"

"It was about what I expected, lots of glitterfolk, drugs, and games. And Lee was his usual kind self."

Johnny frowned. "Nothing else?"

"He asked me to leave the senator and join his organization."

"What did you say?"

"I'd think about it, of course. It wouldn't do to turn him down flat. Besides, I thought stringing him might do us some good. He's a valuable contact, right?"

"Right." Karl nodded.

Johnny said, "What do you think of him as a person?"

"He's not as bad as I'd thought. In fact, I think I like him."

"Don't."

She laughed. "How can I not? He's polite and he's charming, and from what I've seen he's pretty harmless. I think the Disruption made a mistake, listing him as a prime target."

"He's slick, that's all," Johnny said, "like us."

"I think I know him better than you do!"

"That may be the problem."

Shelly sat back, tight-lipped, silent. It was no good talking to Johnny when he got this way, she saw. As long as she knew the truth, it didn't matter; Lee Jones seemed so caught up in the glitterworld that she didn't think he'd be doing much of anything, these days, other than enjoying himself. As long as he kept it that way, she'd tolerate him, or perhaps more than tolerate him.

Karl said, "You're all set for the joint meeting?" looking from one to the other of them.

Johnny laughed and leaned back in his seat. "Of course."

Shelly just nodded curtly.

The aircar began to circle, and through the bulkhead

they could hear the muted voice of their driver, Lang, as he spoke to the SecurNet guards in charge of the complex. Once cleared, they started down.

When they landed on the main building's roof, the hatch swung open and Johnny climbed down first, smiling as usual. Guards in black SecurNet uniforms stood rigidly at attention by the lift doors, and they saluted as Karl stepped down. Karl gave them a congenial wave and they relaxed their stance a bit.

"They're good boys," he said to Shelly with a chuckle. "Would you believe they're on our payroll?"

"SecurNet people?"

He winked. "Money can buy anything. Now quiet; there're bound to be monitors near the lift doors."

She followed as Karl and Johnny walked to the elevator. A car had been called and the doors swung open just as they arrived.

"Keep up the good work," Karl said before the doors closed.

"Yes, sir!" said the guards.

They started down. Shelly studied the brass railings, the small chandelier overhead, the intricate carved woodwork on the walls. *More decadence,* she thought with disgust. In the days of the democracy such waste never would have been tolerated.

Then the doors opened onto a huge circular theater, with row upon row of flowform seats looking down on a broad stage. Most of the seats were already taken, since the meeting was about to start, so Johnny and Karl hustled down to the bottom row, part of which had been reserved for them.

As she leaned back and grew comfortable, Shelly noticed Lee Jones was one of the men seated on stage at the table. He smiled at her and nodded slightly. She replied in kind.

One of the men on stage pounded a gavel. Talk ceased instantly. The man stood and began reading from his notes:

"As you all know, fellow congressmen, this quarter has hit us rather hard. Crime is up over two points over last year, business is in a minor controlled recession, and our South American colonies are falling behind on production quotas. As a result, the originally scheduled bonuses have been reduced by thirty-five percent."

There were murmurs of protest from the floor. The man waited until they quieted down before continuing.

"However, there is cause for optimism. The Central American war is winding down, and vile communism will doubtless be driven from our continent's shores within the year." At that came scattered applause. The man smiled. "As a result, we may soon be adding more colonies, and the governmental bonus on surplus income would cover them as well."

The applause grew wilder.

"Now, I believe we have a number of scheduled reports. I believe Senator Winston is first. Senator?"

Slowly, ponderously, Karl stood. He hooked his thumbs in his daysuit pockets as he turned. "I have good news indeed," he said loudly. The microphones picked up his words and echoed them through the theater.

Shelly looked from Karl to Johnny and back again. What was this? Why hadn't they told her?

Slowly Karl regarded all the gathered senators and representatives, all their aides and associates. He cleared his throat.

"I have news," he said slowly, heavily, "of the terrorist group that calls itself the Disruption. Three years ago I personally selected a team of men for a dangerous, possibly deadly assignment: to infiltrate the terrorists, to gather information on their members and activities, and to report directly to me. Now these national heroes have returned. I wish to call one of them to testify before you. I give you my aide John Zedowski."

Johnny stood. There was a idiot smile on his face, as though he knew what was happening, had expected it. Once again Shelly began to feel the fury of betrayal. She kept it bottled in, listening, praying not to hear what she thought was coming.

Johnny folded his arms behind his back. Then he said:

"As part of an undercover operation initiated by Senator Winston, several undercover agents infiltrated the terrorist organization known as the Disruption. Finally we have a list of all the conspirators involved. Finally we can act. *Now* is the time to end all terrorism, to smash forever this underground network which has plagued us all!"

He produced a paper and began to read. "The current head of the Disruption is Karen Fitzpatrick. Her aides are Carter Smith and Harriet Moretta. Second in command is—"

Shelly listened in shock as Johnny's voice droned on and on, naming the members of cell after cell, all but signing the death order for countless dozens of Disruptionists. Her head hurt. Her stomach tied itself in knots. She could scarcely believe what she was hearing.

Instinctively her hand went for the gun she no longer had. Damn him! She longed to splatter him across half the stage.

Political theory? I believe in rule by the people. Of course a mob cannot rule itself; that's what delegates are for, and that's why the American democracy lasted almost two hundred and fifty years.

—John Zedowski
Asylum

—10—

"**Y**OU bastard," she whispered.

She knew what had happened: power corrupts, and absolute power corrupts absolutely. Johnny'd told her that enough times. Now it had happened to him . . . he'd seen the way Congress lived and he'd liked it. *Longed* for it. Together with Karl he'd plotted to betray the Disruption, destroy everyone who could identify him as an ex-Disruptionist, just so he could stay on and live in the shadow of Congress. He had become one of the people whom he had sworn to destroy.

Silently she cursed him for his weakness. At that instant she saw all the glitterfolk for what they were, knew Lee Jones and his kind could never be for her. She hated them all, hated everything they stood for. They'd taken Harran and Cal from her. Now they'd taken Johnny.

Again she wished for her pistol, a weapon of any kind.

He hadn't yet called her name. She didn't think he would (he owed her that much, at least), but she wasn't taking any chances. It was time to bolt, time to run for cover. She wasn't stupid. She always looked out for herself. If Johnny didn't spill her, someone else from the Disruption might.

She rose, and Karl grabbed her arm.

"Shelly, no—"

"You bastards!" she hissed back, so only he could hear. "Traitors!"

She broke his feeble old-man's grip and pulled away. He would never chase her, never do more than stare after her as she stalked up the aisle toward the lifts, she knew. Karl was Johnny's puppet, just as Johnny was Congress's.

Johnny Zed's voice rolled on behind her, working toward a crescendo. The congressmen watched in fascination. Some, she noticed, were smiling like children. Even the SecurNet guards were drawn up in Johnny's spell.

Shelly entered an elevator car and punched the button for the roof. When the doors opened, she stomped out onto the concrete landingpad. The air was hot, dry, and she felt utterly alone, utterly betrayed. How could they do this to her? How could Johnny and Karl betray the men and women they'd worked beside, struggled beside, for so many years?

Rubbing tears from her eyes, she gazed out across D.C., across the open expanse of lawn dotted here and there with palatial houses. She could never survive alone here, she thought; D.C. wasn't her territory. She needed to get back to centerSprawl. That was her best bet, at least for the moment.

She walked to Karl's aircar. Lang, the chauffeur, saw her coming and popped the hatch. How much did he know? How much was he involved in Johnny's plans? Best not to take any chances, she thought, dropping into one of the seats.

"Where to?" the intercom asked.

"CenterSprawl. Jalto Junction."

"Right." The intercom clicked off.

The aircar rose smoothly, turning north, heading for the Sprawl. She looked out the window. The ground below blurred and took on an air of unreality as the repeller fields extended to full power.

The Junction, Shelly thought, would be the perfect place to lose herself: dozens of transit lines came together there, platforms and bullet trains and even the local subways. It always bustled. Nobody could follow her trail through such a mess. She'd be miles away before Johnny Zed even finished his speech.

Her mind was racing, plotting schemes too wild, too complex to ever work. Assassinating Johnny and Karl ... destroying Congress ... wiping them and their Sirencall of power from the face of America ...

Slowly reality caught up with her. She specialized in weapons, not tactics, not technology. Without Johnny and Karl, she didn't have many options.

The feet have my blood. And Johnny could have her name up on every SecurNet board in the country. ...

She needed an organization, that much was clear. She needed the Disruption ... or something similar. She bit her lip. If the Disruption truly *were* gone now, surely that left a power vacuum. She'd studied enough social dynamics to realize that. And, where a vacuum existed, another organization might arise, a new movement to replace the old.

She saw it all, suddenly, in a flash of inspiration. Small independent cells working together to destroy Congress, and no mere Disruption this time, but violent revolution.

She could lead them. She had the experience, the ambition, the hate to drive them. It could succeed!

But first she needed friends, allies, people to back her. A few Disruptionists would doubtless escape the congressional arrests. And there would be former members, men and women who'd bolted from the Disruption early on, men and women who'd burned out on revolution and taken off to lose themselves in the pabulum of the masses. People such as Cal.

If Johnny Zed wanted the Disruption destroyed, let him believe it . . . until her new band was ready to strike.

"The word," she whispered, hot, angry, "is *revenge*."

She flipped on the vid to catch the NewsNets. They were giving the Disruption prime coverage. Again and again Johnny's speech was played, with Congress clapping and cheering every step of the way.

It wasn't like that, she thought. *The vids have changed what happened.*

And Johnny was a national hero. And Congress was happy. And the Disruption was dying.

The roundup of Disruptionists had started. Scenes of violence flared on the screen: a firefight between SecurNet troops and Disruptionists in the Tartown District . . . bombs exploding in Fishtown as Disruptionists destroyed computer records, and themselves . . . and there were pitched battles in the streets, snipers on roofs, gunfire and bombings and gas attacks—

Shelly wept a bit as the SecurNet tallies scrolled past. Three hundred fifty-four captured. One thousand eighty-two dead.

Her people were being slaughtered, and the Disruption with them. Congress's victory was complete.

The intercom crackled. "The turbostation is temporarily closed to air traffic and there are riots in the streets," Lang said. "There is rioting throughout Jalto Junction. Are you certain I can't set you down in the secured area?"

Rioting? Shelly looked out the window. Smoke from dozens of fires hazed the sky, and she could see masses of people swarming through a few of the streets, smashing windows, throwing bricks, fighting and looting. *It's just as well*, she thought. *They'll only make it harder for Johnny to follow me*.

She said: "Pick a clear area and put me down there."

"As you wish. From the smoke I would suggest you take a respirator from the storage compartment."

"Thanks." She untabbed the little closet, found it stocked with survival equipment. Dumping it out onto the floor, she rifled through it . . . respirators, flares, a spare radio, two mace grenades . . . and, at the very back of the compartment hanging on little hooks, a pistol. She took it out. It was a Magus .35, loaded with twelve bullets. After checking the safety, she tucked it into her pocket, then stood.

The aircar touched ground with a slight jolt. She steadied herself against the wall, then pulled on a respirator and unsealed the hatch.

They were on a residential street, with apartment buildings stretching as far into the smoky haze as she could see. When she hopped to the ground, the heat hit her, and the humidity. She could feel sweat begin to trickle down her face, her neck, her back. Far off she heard screams and shouting, followed by the sound of breaking glass.

"Are you *certain* you want out here?" Lang asked again.

In reply Shelly palmed the handpad; the hatch resealed itself. Turning, she hiked up the street, away from the worst sounds of violence and looting. This section of the Sprawl, it seemed, had gone to riot.

She turned at the first corner. Ahead fires burned, and smoke rolled down the street, rippling, curling in banks like fog. Through the haze Shelly could see the soft blue-green-red glow of neon. The looters had already passed, she thought; it would be safe for now.

She thumbed the respirator's filter up to high and walked

into the worst of the smoke. The buildings ahead were vague, indistinct, but she recognized them: the turbostation lay only a few blocks ahead.

From the corner of her eye she glimpsed movement. It was enough to set her nerves on edge. Ever so slightly, she turned her head. A gray catman, she saw, young and sleekly feline, paralleled her course. He turned his head, and his eyes caught the light and shone like little bits of amber. There was a silver band on his head and he seemed to be speaking in a low voice. A radio?

Shelly stopped. The catman stopped, too, sitting back on his haunches. Slowly he lifted one paw, licked it. His eyes never left her face.

Whatever the catman was up to, Shelly didn't like it. She turned and walked on. Putting her hands in her pockets, she felt the smooth hardness of her .35 and flicked off the safety.

Again the catman paced her, keeping close watch, talking in a voice so low she couldn't hear it. Finally she stopped, whirled to face him.

"What the hell do you want?" she demanded.

He sat again, and again he licked his paw.

"Well?" she demanded, taking a step forward. "Speak quick, pussycat. Haven't got all day."

His tail lashed once. Then his head jerked to the right and he seemed to smile a bit.

Shelly followed his gaze. Large shapes drifted in the haze, pacing back and forth, back and forth like caged animals. Finally they moved forward, and she found herself looking at several dozen catmen. At the head of the pack stood two she recognized: one gold, one black. Neither looked very happy.

The established order will always take part in overthrowing itself, from inciting the peasants to joining the revolutionaries to leading the attack on their own homes...it is the nature of things.

—John Zedowski
Asylum

—11—

SHELLY felt her fingers tighten around the pistol in her pocket.

"I've got a gun," she said. Her voice rasped through the respirator. "Pass me by or I'll waste you cold this time."

Manlike the gold catman reared up, and she could see from the way his ears laid back, from the way his whiskers twitched, that hate boiled within him. His cat-pawed hands jerked, gestured, claws like glittery steel knives cutting through the air.

Human voiced he said: "We have been watching for you."

"So."

"Catkind takes care of its own."

"You started the quarrel. End it. Let me pass."

Laughing he flowed onto all fours once more, pacing

back and forth, and his claws click-click-clicked against the street's pavement. The other catmen, half hidden in the smoke, clicked their claws, too, until the sound echoed at her from every direction.

"You've been warned," Shelly said. Hardening her expression, she stared straight at the gold catman and strode toward him. Tension made her shoulders tight, her back ache with the strain. Why was he doing this to her? She had a gun. She'd knocked his ribs in once and she could do it again. She could kill him this time, even with his friends on the ready. Couldn't he see she had him set and match?

As she'd dreaded, the catman sat on his haunches, tail flicking behind him, and met her gaze unblinkingly. He was daring her on, daring her to fight. There was a cocksure madness in him, combined with the pain of humiliation.

Shit. There's no way left but to fight. Shelly didn't miss a step. She kept the pistol in her pocket aimed at the catman's chest. A .35 would make a mess at this range no matter where she hit him, but that didn't concern her. More important, what would the other catmen do if she killed their leader? Hopefully they'd ditch him. *Catkind takes care of its own.* Not a good thought.

The gold catman rose and made a mock leap at her, tail lashing, growling from deep in his throat. He was in, then away, dancing, prancing, taunting. He hadn't come nearly close enough to touch her, at least not yet. It was a game, him toying with her. What had Karl called it? *Deathplay.*

Grim, Shelly kept walking. Smoke swirled around her, thicker here, like the folds of a cloak, and she could no longer see the other catmen. The world narrowed down to the gold catman and her, him dancing before her, hypnotizing her with his movements. He stared into her eyes now and she tried to stare him down, found she couldn't. There was such hatred within him, such bloodlust, that she knew he could never let her pass alive.

Only twelve bullets, she thought. *Got to make every shot.*

Suddenly the catman crouched. *This is it,* she thought, nerves jumping. Time slowed. Muscles bunched, the catman sprang, blurred gold. He hung in the air for an eternity.

Shelly shot through the pocket of her coat. The bullet tore into the catman's belly, knocking him yowling back in the air. He twisted and tried to bite the wound.

And then his body exploded with a dull *whump* and a flash of red light, and little bits of him sprayed in all directions, gobs of bloody fur and splintered bones and bits of intestine like overcooked sausage. The blood flew across Shelley's goggles and she wiped at it mechanically, smearing it.

When she could see again, everything hazed in pink, she gaped in shock at what was left of the gold catman: a shapeless lump of fur surrounded by radiating spikes of blood, a sunburst done all in crimson. The scene had an oddly surreal element to it, through the blood-smeared goggles, as though she were watching a vid rather than real life. A buzzing filled her ears, and she could feel her heart beating in her throat. She could smell the blood, too, thick and sweet; even the respirator couldn't cut it out. Distantly she realized the bullet must have been tipped with an explosive. She just hadn't noticed when she'd checked the weapon. She wanted to puke.

For a second she just stood there. Then a bit of wind blew the smoke past and she could see the other catmen again, all of them sitting and staring at the leader's remains, horrified, unbelieving. A collective wail came up, a piercing, moaning shriek of anguish.

It cut through the fog in Shelly's mind. Slowly she

turned, looking them over. There were dozens of them now, she saw, thirty or forty at least. Eyes glittering, they mourned their lost companion.

Smoke drifted around her again. She didn't hesitate. Skirting the remains of the gold catman's body, she headed for the turbostation at a brisk walk. Any faster and they might give chase at once; any slower and she might not get away.

A silence rose behind her. Shelly shivered. From the corners of her eyes she saw shapes drifting phantomlike through the smoke to either side, and then again she could hear the telltale click of metal claws on pavement.

With no show of subtlety, she drew and cocked the pistol. If they wanted to fight, she'd let them know what they were in for. Eleven bullets with explosive tips could do a hell of a lot of damage, and she intended killing as many as possible, if they forced a fight.

She saw the turbostation clearly now, its brilliant lights cutting like beacons through the haze. *I'll make it,* she thought then. *They're not going to attack. They*—

And as she thought it, they hit her from all sides at once, a tsunami of leaping, slashing, clawing, mewing fur. Shelly tried to duck and roll, managed to get out from the worst of their mass. Something burned her head and stomach, her arms and chest. She whirled, finger jerking the trigger again and again, firing into bellies, into faces. Flesh exploded; blood and fur sprayed everywhere, across her face, across her goggles, blinding her. Then they were all on her, clawing and snapping, and she was emptying the last of her clip into them—and punching, screaming, scrambling for cover herself—

Silence. Just as suddenly it was over. Pain from wounds niggled at the back of her mind; more pressing was the heavy weight on her chest.

She pushed off what felt like a half-dozen catmen, then

hunched over on hands and knees. Her chest hurt and she still couldn't draw a full breath. It was the respirator, she realized suddenly, and she jerked it off. The filter was clogged with bloody fur. She'd never get it clean.

She heaved it away from her as hard as she could, watched it skitter down the street a good twenty meters. Taking a series of deep, half-panting breaths, she emptied her mind, forced herself to unkey. The air tasted dry and sooty, but at least she could breathe now. At least she was still alive.

After wiping her face on her coat's lining, she felt infinitely better. Her arms and legs were covered with claw marks, some deep, most just scratches, and her hair was matted with still more blood from a scalp cut. It stung like hell, but it could have been much, much worse.

She stood unsteadily. There were two headless corpses at her feet, and a half-dozen others scattered around her, all red and twisted and looking like ground meat. Groaning a bit, she looked away. She could remember the last time she'd felt this bad. It was the night Harran died.

Slowly she looked up and down the street. The rest of the catmen had gone, had fled into the shadows, dragging the wounded with them. *Catkind takes care of its own.* Shuddering again, she turned and meandered on. She wished she'd never heard of modified people, not Cal, not even Johnny Zed. They were cee-pure trouble.

By the time she neared the turbostation, the whole evening had taken on a further air of unreality. Johnny betraying the Disruption . . . catmen attacking her . . . this sort of thing just didn't happen in real life! A few hours ago she'd had ideas, plans that had seemed so easy to carry out. Now she'd lost those proud thoughts; her schemes seemed tattered and ruined. With them gone, her drive and conviction melted away as well; all she wanted to do was crawl into a hole for the rest of her life.

The lights drew brighter as she plodded onward, feet leaden. The smoke lessened and she found the air clear; looters hadn't been this way. Finally she saw the reason why: the feet had set up a barricade of aircars to guard the turbostation.

She didn't care anymore. She walked through the feet lines as though she belonged, and when a couple of uniformed officers hustled up to her, she just looked at them with a hurt, pathetic expression.

"I'll take that," one of them said as he eased the pistol from her hand.

She looked at it; she hadn't realized she was still carrying it. Then she looked at the feet. They were both middle-aged, going to fat, tired eyes red and dark-lined. It had been a long evening for them, too, she could tell. She couldn't even muster a feeling of hatred and disgust.

"Yes," she said.

"What happened?" the other one asked. He had a note-pad in his hand.

"Catmen," she said, sounding shocked, bewildered. "They tried to kill me."

The feet nodded as he took notes. "I've heard of that before. Bloodsport, they call it. Nothing to worry about now, though. You're safe here, Miss . . . ?"

"Gluckman, Patty Gluckman."

He wrote that down, too. "The government set up a Red Cross platform inside. They'll get your wounds treated and you cleaned up, Miss Gluckman."

"Thank you," she whispered. It was easy, so easy to fall into the role of helpless young woman.

"You don't want to make a report and file charges, do you?"

"No."

He laughed hard. "Yeah, didn't think so. From the looks of you, there ain't much left of them to press charges *against*." Still chuckling, he turned to the other feet. "Yo, Biff, why don't you escort her in to the RC and get her taken care of?"

Two hours later she'd been cleaned up by the Red Cross, her wounds stitched and plastifleshed, the pain of countless scratches and bites tranqued to a subtle ache with eeztabs. Everyone was unbearably nice to her the whole time, and when they thought she wasn't looking, she saw how they whispered about her and shook their heads sadly at "the catmen and their random attacks." She was just a victim, after all, one of dozens in the RC station, and the nurses had seen it all before.

Finally Shelly felt put together enough to leave. Her thoughts were lucid, calm for the first time since she'd left Congress. She knew what she had to do. Wounded, with everyone from the catmen to the feet to Johnny and Secur-Net out to get her, she only had one choice: bolt.

And she had one bolt-hole left, a place even Johnny didn't know about. She hated to use it, but this time the circumstances warranted.

Home.

She used most of her in-hand cash for the platform ticket, then settled back to wait on an empty bench. It was growing dark, and the emptiness of the turbostation mirrored the emptiness within her. All sane people were home right now, watching the evening vids, letting the feet and the SecurNet forces do the cleanup work.

Home. That's where she'd be in two hours. It was an unpleasant thought.

An hour later, the Sprawl was a glow of light on the horizon. Dark fields slipped away below, and carefully groomed forests, and between them endless rows of identical little houses, each one floodlit for the night in pastel pinks and yellows and greens. She hadn't been home since she'd run off with Cal to join the Disruption five years before. Would Mother and Dad still have her? She thought so. They were set in their ways; it would be just like them to take her back, to forgive her for running away. Perhaps they'd even dreamed of her return, she as their good little girl become repentant after wild years. Well, that's what she'd give them . . . at least for a time.

Finally she saw huge, kidney-shaped Nixon Lake glimmering faintly with starlight. *Almost there*. The platform dropped down, and she pulled herself over to the exit ramp.

She was the only one to get off at this stop. The station, little more than a large slab of concrete, hadn't changed a bit in five years. It still had the same advertising posters in the ticket office's windows, the same row of vending machines against the back wall.

She headed north up Reagan Road. The walk from the station seemed longer and more painful than ever before, and she was more than glad of the darkness: there would be no prying neighbors to see her, to come out and click their tongues and offer her lifts to her house in their shiny new Caddils. Just wait a minute while I put papers down on the aircar seat, dear: don't want blood all over everything, do we?

Finally she reached the proper white picket fence, swung open the gate, walked between two perfect flower beds to the front door. The eeztabs had worn off; she felt raw pain pulsing at her temples, through her wounds.

Staggering a bit, she put her hand on the pad, and a bit to her surprise the door buzzed briefly, then unlocked itself. Leave it to her parents to trust her to come home. Softly she pushed it open and went into the dimly lit foyer.

The place still smelled the same, warm and faintly musty, and it still had little pictures of Shelly and Jeanie and Karen in the knickknack cabinet, next to ceramic sculptures of birds and dogs and horses. A glance at the opticon brightened the lights and she could see the same gray throwrugs on the hardwood floors. Nothing had changed at all. Nothing ever did in the burbs.

"Mother? Dad?"

Distantly, she could hear the vid playing in the living room. Grimacing a bit at a stitch in her side, she went up the two small steps to the hallway, past the roses on the vidtape case, past the faded watercolors of butterflies and birds she and her sisters had done in school.

She paused in the doorway. Two people sat in the living room, both gray haired, one knitting as she watched a game-show, the other just watching as he rocked in his comfortable old chair.

"Mother," Shelly whispered, "Dad." Her head was ringing and she felt hot all over. And then her legs gave out and there was only darkness.

When she woke, she was pleasantly warm, and it was hard to persuade herself to open her eyes. When she did, it was to pink wallpaper and a white ceiling. A shelf along the far wall held stuffed animals she recognized, teddy bears mostly, but also a few dogs and a pair of gray-green dinosaurs. "Ilya and Petrov," she said, remembering them with a touch of affection. It had been so long. . . .

"It's all right, dear."

Shelly turned her head. Her mother sat beside her, smiling faintly, looking concerned and reassuring at once. There were a few more lines around her eyes, and her hair was frosted whiter than it had been, but little else seemed different. She even wore the same deep red NuFur robe she'd worn every night for the last twenty years.

"What happened?"

"You fainted. Little wonder, considering the state you're in. I declare, I've never seen anyone as cut up as you!"

"Catmen did it."

"First thing tomorrow we'll go down to the police station and file a complaint against them. We can't have things like that happening around here!"

"I've filed a complaint already. It happened in the Sprawl."

"Dear me." She shook her head sadly. "I don't know what this world's coming to."

Shelly nodded. "If it's all right with you, I'd like to stay here for a few weeks, rest up, recover."

"Of course. Now rest, Shelly dear. That's the best thing for you. We'll have the doctor in to look at you bright and early tomorrow morning, when you're feeling stronger."

Shelly started to protest, then thought better of it and smiled and nodded. "I think that's a good idea." It wouldn't do to argue with her mother, not here, not while she needed this place as a sanctuary. Tomorrow was a long time off, and things could easily change by then.

Rising, her mother kissed her on the forehead, then left, pulling the door closed. Shelly could hear her walking down the hall, toward the stairs.

Quickly Shelly sat up. The vid's remote control was on the bedside table. She grabbed it and started flicking through the channels, finally stopping when she came to a NewsNet covering the Sprawl.

". . . terrorist network known as the Disruption is finally broken," the newscaster said pleasantly, "thanks to the heroic work of Senator Winston and his chief aide, John Zedowski. An estimated nineteen hundred members of the Disruption were rounded up earlier this afternoon by SecurNet forces throughout the country." [Scenes of SecurNet troops pouring out of aircars, shoot-outs with men and women Shelly half-recognized, firebombings and gassings.] "Although a few Disruptionists remain at large, Congress has all their names and descriptions. It's only a matter of time before their capture."

"Shit," Shelly said, knowing it was true.

"In a related story, Joseph Gilford, the self-proclaimed leader of the Disruption, died at his own hands in Paris this evening." [A picture of the Eiffel Tower, then a cut to the outside of a building, then inside to a sheet-covered body on a linoleum floor.] "Already congressional leaders are calling this the end of terrorism in the United States. Once again, America is free of the scourge known as the Disruption."

Karl—Senator Winston—appeared on the screen. He smiled into the camera, saying, "It's a proud day for all Americans."

Shelly trembled, fighting back tears. Gilford was dead. Suicide was the easy way out; she'd expected more from him. Hadn't he once said, "Suicide is the fool's escape. It takes a smart man to stay alive in the face of adversity, to work calmly and competently until he reaches his goal." Thus another of her dreams was punctured; Gilford had been as weak as any other man.

The NewsNet went on and on in the same vein for the next two hours, showing more pictures of violence, broadcasting the names and pictures of Disruptionists still at large. Shelly listened and watched all the more carefully, but no mention of her was made. She found her omission doubly ominous. She should have been in the Disruption's files, which SecurNet captured before they could be destroyed, and she should have been in Johnny's report. Or had he somehow managed to protect her, as she'd first thought he would? Or were they withholding her name deliberately, so she'd think herself safe and come back to light? That was devious, like Johnny. Yes. They'd be waiting to pounce like spiders . . . like catmen . . . when she showed.

Another datum angered her: John Zedowski had been named deputy minister of civil intelligence by congressional acclamation. That put him high up among Congress's appointed positions, in charge of most of SecurNet's forces. What he could do with all that power at his command . . .

Shelly couldn't bear to watch anymore. Angrily she flicked off the vid, settled back in bed. There were tears on her cheeks and an emptiness inside her that no fleshly wound had caused.

When Shelly woke the next morning, she had a blinding headache. On top of that, her every muscle ached with its own private pain—a further insult, since she'd believed herself in good shape. Groaning a bit, she eased herself to her feet, found her way to the bathroom. Inside the medicine chest were several packets of eeztabs; she felt marginally better after she'd slapped a couple against her temples.

She spent the whole day lying abed watching the News-Nets while her mother bustled about and tried to make everything more comfortable, all the time grating on Shelly's nerves. Shelly wished her parents could somehow be less patronizing, less predictable—less like the sheep they were. She loved them, but she fully recognized their weaknesses: if things had been any different five years earlier, she might not have felt compelled to run away with Cal, might not have tried to change things for the better. If only . . .

She watched feet and SecurNet forces round up the last few of her companions-in-arms. Each arrest sounded another death knell for the Disruption. The fight was over, and she knew it as surely as she'd ever known anything. There couldn't be more than a handful of Disruptionists still around. She'd never be able to dig them out by herself.

Dinner was an elegant five-course meal whipped up on the spur of the moment by the autochef, and afterward Shelly's parents wanted her to watch vids with them. Instead, she retired early, pleading exhaustion. Her parents didn't object. Shelly tranqued herself to sleep.

So the next few weeks went. Shelly never left the house, preferring to take things slowly as her wounds healed. At last even the deepest cuts vanished to scars. She could stretch and not feel sharp pains across her arms and back. Still she waited, watching the vid, growing sleepy with her parents and falling into the routine of burber life.

A month later, dressed in an old gray daysuit, Shelly came down to breakfast as usual. Her mother was up and about already, polishing the chrome on the autochef, on all the latest cooking equipment. She barely looked up as Shelly slipped into her seat at the table.

"I asked some of your old friends to stop by," her mother said with a serene smile. "I knew you'd want to see them."

Shelly didn't. They were shallow, empty creatures, worse even than her parents, and her boredom with them had been another part of what drove her to Cal, to the Disruption. She would have been happier never meeting any of them again.

Instead, "Which friends?" she asked reluctantly.

"Janis and Gloria. They'll be here any minute to take you to the mall. I remember how you used to like it so. . . ."

Shelly sighed. "Yes, mother." She was a guest here, she had to remind herself. This was a refuge, a last place to hide. She couldn't afford to alienate her parents.

"That's a good girl. Oh, and Shelly, since I don't know where you were working, I told them you were a hairdresser, and that you'd come home to see us on your vacation." She shook her head. "What *do* you do now, Shelly dear? I certainly wish you'd call more often to keep us up-to-date."

"That's fine, Mother. I'm a hairdresser."

"Good, good." She nodded as she wandered over to the shining chrome stove.

The autochef smiled down on her. "It's almost lunchtime," he said cheerfully. "Ready to start cooking? I am!"

"Yes? Why, so it is!" she said. She seemed a bit flustered. "We'd better get started right away. Now," she said, turning back to Shelly and making little shooing motions with her hands, "you run along and have fun, dear."

Janis and Gloria hadn't changed. They pulled up to the house in the latest model Skybird, painted hot pink. It was the most expensive luxury personal aircar available, barely fifteen feet long, with chrome gleaming along its every line.

Janis popped the door and climbed out, smoothing her shimmering green dress. Her hair and eyes had been dyed green to match, and she wore glowing green lipstick.

Shelly came out to meet her halfway. "Hello!" she called, waving. "Long time!"

"Slay me, babes!" said Janis, grinning. Her teeth were green, too. "Looksee wherezat, comer? Wow, like hair!"

"Yeah," Shelly said, scarcely understanding. "Hair's it, right?" Burbspeak seemed to have drifted far beyond what it had been before she left. She linked arms with her old friend and let Janis lead her back to the aircar.

Shelly climbed in next to Gloria, who was done over entirely in pink to match the aircar, then settled back for the ride. Janis was babbling on about hairdressers, and as long as Shelly kept smiling and nodding and agreeing every now and then, everyone seemed content.

"Babes, we'll mallwait for friends!" Gloria said, laughing. "Gang's backslashed for you." And Janis laughed at that, too, and neither one would say any more during the ride.

Shelly had an odd feeling they'd planned a surprise for her, and she wasn't sure she'd like it.

It took twenty minutes to reach the mall, and when they arrived and pulled into Gloria's private aircar slot, half a dozen people were already waiting: all mall workers dressed in neat gray uniforms.

As Shelly stepped down from the aircar, they seized her arms and propelled her despite her protests and struggles toward the service door.

Distantly she heard Gloria calling, "Slicker, babes, makeover's coming!" Then the mallmen slapped sleeptabs onto her cheeks and she became woozy, passed out.

What is the price of discontent? Revolution. And what is the price of revolution? Discontent. It's a vicious circle.

—John Zedowski
Revolution Today

—12—

WHEN she woke, Shelly felt good, better than she'd felt in a long time. She lay there with her eyes closed, listening to soft waterfall-like music. She felt as if she'd just been to a bodyshop and gotten all the latest upgrades, her new nerves tingling and alive, her senses heightened.

She opened her eyes and found herself lying in the dark on a sensubed. It pushed and rubbed at her back, massaging, vibrating ever so faintly. It was a decadent toy, one she found all too easy to enjoy.

Gritting her teeth, she sat up. She couldn't let herself become like her old friends, just another mindless burber living for the joy of mechanized society. Determined to leave and not waste another second, she pushed aside gauze curtains and swung her legs to the floor. She stood, barefoot, on deep carpeting. It was still dark, but she could hear the rustle of other people on sensubeds around her. Which way was the door? She took a guess and started forward, arms outstretched. Before she'd taken three steps she stumbled over a body.

"Upside, babes!" she heard Gloria say. "Feetwatch! Makeover cool?"

"Yeah." Whatever. "Which way's out?"

Giggles from several different directions. Then there were hands on her hands, guiding her fingers to her forehead. She was wearing glasses of some kind, she found, pushed up high. She pulled them into place and suddenly she could see again, all in shades of pink. *Infrared,* she realized.

There were perhaps a dozen of her old friends in the senstim chamber, all tranqued out on custom drugs. Their eyes were almost completely black behind their goggles, pupils dilated so big the slightest flash of day would have blinded them. From the feel of her own body—the heightened senses, the tingling skin—Shelly guessed she was tranqued out, too, her pupils big and black as theirs. They had her effectively trapped with them, these burber glitterfolk: she saw it all now, the setup her mother and father and ex-friends had planned. They all wanted her back with them, again the obedient daughter, again one of a crowd of giggling teenagers.

When Shelly looked at Gloria and Janis and Belle and the rest, she still saw the same sixteen-year-old faces behind the layers of makeup and bodyshop alterations. They, too, could have been part of a conspiracy of sameness, a vast plot to keep the status quo. Or perhaps paranoia was a side effect of the drugs she was on? Shelly shivered. Most likely there had been no conscious decision on anyone's part to try to trap her here, with her old friends and her old life. Most likely it had just . . . *happened*, a part of the uncontrollable flood of human events, another sign of the degeneracy of the American public.

And yet . . . it would be so easy to let them do it to her, to once more become a member of their little clique. The glitterfolk weren't so bad. She remembered Lee Jones and his friends, how much fun she'd had with them at that private party . . . all the games, all the laughing, all the feelings she'd had of finally *belonging*. Here was the same chance again; she could stay in the burbs, laughing and playing with her old friends, living with her parents. She could get a job, perhaps as a hairdresser—

She shivered. *No,* she thought, *that's the drugs thinking, not me. How can I leave Johnny with his triumph?*

She pushed her way through her friends. She could see the door now, outlined with thin blades of white light, and there was a tall, muscular attendant beside it.

He caught her hand as she reached for the pad. She almost broke his arm, but restrained herself.

"Don't go out, miss," he said. "The light would hurt your eyes."

Her eyes . . . yes, dilated so big they'd be sensitive to day. She'd almost forgotten. For now she'd have to stay with her old friends and their games. But she wouldn't join them, she swore, and when the drugs wore off, she'd ditch them, go back to the Sprawl, back to a life that actually meant something.

It was as though she'd awakened from a dream. How could she have possibly thought of giving up all she'd worked and fought for? How could she have almost given up on the Disruption? Though Gilford was gone, his dream would live. That was her life. It had to be her goal.

She lay back on a sensubed, feathers and pillows flying all around her, the laughter of her friends ringing emptily in her ears. Yes. It was time to draw up sides. It was time to fight.

The first step would be putting together a new cell. She would be the new revolution's heart, its leader and guiding force, at least in the beginning. But to carry out her plans she'd need help: technical boys like Johnny, tacticians like Karl... or like Cal.

What had happened to Cal after he'd burned out? She shivered a bit as she thought of his dog-whiskered face brushing against hers, how much she'd loved him. Where would he have gone? He'd always talked of his New England childhood with an odd longing. Perhaps there. It would certainly be the place to start. How far could he have run in the five years since she'd last seen him? Not far enough to escape her.

And she knew his real name. It had been the ultimate show of his faith in her, of his trust. He'd been just Cal Fornia to the Disruption; to her he'd always be Calvin Drake.

Finally, six hours later, when she crashed from her high and felt human again, she found out what her friends had ordered for her makeover. She had frizzy glowing-orange hair, pale orange lips, and umber fingernails. It made her look like a teenager again, she thought, studying the effect. Fat had been injected into the wrinkles around her eyes and lips; her complexion was smooth as a baby's. Unwittingly it seemed they'd done her a favor, provided her with a disguise so perfect even Johnny would have had a hard time recognizing her on a crowded street. It was just the disguise she needed to go out into the world once more.

As their little crowd pushed out into the mall proper, they babbled on about fashion and flashrock and other things in which Shelly had no interest. She made no pretense of sticking with them. Instead, she turned to the right and strolled off alone, ignoring puzzled shouts behind her.

For a time they followed her, talking among themselves,

giggling, but when she entered an aircar rental agency they gave up and wandered off. Glitterfolk had short attention spans; they needed something to dazzle their senses every few minutes, Shelly knew, or they grew bored. And she'd bored them.

Smiling, she stepped up to the rental desk. "I want a small aircar," she said to the gray-uniformed woman on duty.

"Certainly. Colored to match your hair?"

"No. Black."

"Ah, yes, basic black is always popular this time of year. Which account shall I bill?"

"I'll pay cash. I only need it for a day."

"Certainly, certainly. Put your print here."

A section of the countertop became a transparent square. Shelly palmed it. It flared with a hot white light that made her hand tingle. Then the square faded away.

The woman was holding a gray plastic chit. "Here. Go to the main entrance; a boy will bring it around for you."

The trip back to the Sprawl took two hours. As she let the autopilot drive, she took quick stock of her situation.

On the negative side she had no weapons, no organization to back her, and nobody she could trust. On the plus side, she had a bit over a thirty thousand 'dollars in cash—her mother must have put it in her pocket while she slept, an incentive to go wild in the mall with her friends—and she had a plan for restarting a revolution that began with finding Cal. She also had a firm goal in life: destroying Congress, Johnny Zed, and all they stood for. That alone was enough to keep her going. She could imagine Johnny's laughing, gloating face as he thought of all he'd done to betray the Disruption.

While the aircar flew, she began calling up vidphone directories for New England. There were three Calvin

Drakes listed in the first one, seven in the second, and two more in the third. She sighed and kept scanning. After an hour, she had a list of forty-nine possibilities.

She hadn't thought Calvin or Drake all that common of a name. Well, best to get started; the sooner she found him, the sooner they'd be back in business.

The first Calvin Drake turned out to be a black doctor; the second, a balding plumber; the third, a boy of perhaps ten; the fourth, a smiling insurance salesman who offered her premium fire insurance at a discount. And so it went until she reached the forty-first name, when a small man in a green robe answered.

"I'm trying to reach Cal Drake," Shelly said.

"Why is this?"

"I'm an old friend of his."

"He no longer associates with his old friends."

Her eyes narrowed. "Why not?"

"He is a holy man now. In his third year at the Temple of the Sacred Plant, the gods touched him and made him holy. Please, you must not call here again. Yes."

He severed the connection.

This holy man Cal Drake had been there over three years. That might well fit; Cal always had been a believer, first in Congress, then in the Disruption when Congress proved a failure to him. And now perhaps he was a believer in this Sacred Plant, whatever that was. It was a slim lead, but the best she had for the moment.

Quickly she ran through the remaining numbers. None of them proved correct. That only left number forty-one.

Fortunately, the Temple of the Sacred Plant was listed in the Rhode Island directory. She punched the grid coordinates into the autopilot and settled back for the ride.

When the autopilot signalled their approach, Shelly took the aircar to manual and brought it in low, cruising a scant

meter above street level. She was in an old residential section, full of rambling three-story houses with walls around
them. Straight ahead, at the end of the block, stood a huge
stone wall with rusted iron spikes along the top; domed
buildings covered in gold leaf thrust behind it. That had to
be the temple.

Shelly geared down and set the aircar's repeller fields
whirring. The car practically leaped over the fence. There
was a clearing large enough, so she set down by the wall.

When she popped the front hatch, she found herself facing a dozen men in bright green robes. All of them held
gardening equipment—rakes, shears, shovels. None of
them was smiling, but none looked all that hostile, either.

"Um, hello," Shelly said. She kept her hands in the
open, where they could see them. "Take me to your
leader."

"There are no leaders here," several of the men said.
They stared at her with a strange intensity, and Shelly
found herself shifting uneasily.

Another said, "There are only holy men, and those who
would follow their ways of tranquility."

"I want to see Cal Drake."

"Come with me, please," someone said behind her.

Shelly turned to find the small, dark man she'd spoken
with on the vidphone. Stepping forward, he took her arm.
As he tugged her toward the gold-domed building, the
others returned to their gardening.

"What's your name?" Shelly asked.

"Oak. You will be Carrot."

"Sure, if that will get me in to see Cal."

"There is no longer anyone here by that name. The one
you seek is Willow."

"Willow. Sure."

She followed him through a curtain of blue beads into a
small, dim room. Seated cross-legged in the center of the

room, on a large pillow, was an emaciated old man wearing only a loin cloth.

"This is Carrot," Oak announced solemnly. "She is seeking enlightenment."

She looked around the room for Cal but saw him nowhere. When she turned to demand an explanation of the dark man, she caught the barest glimpse of him disappearing through the bead curtain.

"May I help you, my child?" the old man asked.

Shelly sighed. "I'm looking for Cal Drake," she said. "I was told he was here."

"I was Cal Drake once, my child, but all that was him has passed beyond the fields we know."

"You?" Shelly laughed. "The Cal I knew was a dogman, a burnout."

Something crossed his face for an instant, a look of almost recognition. "Shel?" he whispered.

It was like a cold knife through her heart. "Cal?" she whispered, unbelieving. She stepped closer, then ran and dropped to her knees before him. Up close, she recognized him. His face wasn't wrinkled but scarred, and the scars, she saw, came from where his dog-whiskers had been brutally yanked out. Nothing short of a pair of pliers could have done it, and she found herself almost weeping at the thought of the pain it must have caused him.

She cupped his face in her hands, tried to pull him to her, to comfort him. But Cal only smiled and raised his hands to hold her at a distance.

"I am a holy man now," he said. "The spirits of the fields have touched me. I know only the ways of plants. All is peaceful, and I am happy."

"They've mindwiped you," she said, shocked.

He shook his head. "No. Never would we dream of injuring the flesh."

"That isn't the Cal I know speaking."

His smile was enigmatic. "No. I am Willow now, strong in the wind, with roots to hold me steady in times of trouble. I am no longer à burnout, Carrot, as you put it. I have purpose. I am content."

"How can you be?" She gestured vaguely at all around her. "This . . ."

"It is all that I need."

"Remember the Disruption," she said urgently. "Remember the promise you once made me. You said you'd always be there if I needed you."

"I'm sorry. I have no memory of that." He smiled, and his eyes no longer held their old fire. He was an empty, broken man. "Come," he said, patting the mat beside him. "Sit with me. Let us speak of plants and the ways of Mother Earth. Join us here, Carrot, and you too will find true happiness."

Feeling sick at her stomach, Shelly rose. Cal, her old Cal, was gone, replaced by this *holy man*. It was sickening. He'd been so strong, so confident; how could he have fallen into anything so banal as plant worship? It had to be a mindwipe. Whoever'd recruited him for this church must've done it. They'd taken all the fight out of him. Well, she'd always said religion was for the weak and the mindwiped. *But Cal—*

She didn't want to see him this way. Turning, she almost ran through the curtain of beads, into the antechamber. It was deserted. Coming from outside, though, she heard rough, unpeaceful voices. Those voices, she realized, couldn't possibly belong to the Temple members.

Instincts took over. She reached for a gun that wasn't there, cursed, then pressed herself against the wall beside a window. Cautiously she eased forward and peered out.

There were two feet looking at her aircar, checking its license number against something one of them held. Her stomach jerked spasmodically. Somehow, they'd managed to track her down. Perhaps through her handprint, she thought with dismay. After a month she'd thought the search for Disruptionists would have died down. It seemed Johnny hadn't been kind enough to leave her name off his hitlist after all.

Feigning indifference, she turned and walked back into Cal's room. Cal's eyes were closed and he seemed to be meditating, swaying slowly back and forth. She said nothing; passing him, she went out the back door, into yet another garden. This one was less well groomed than the others; roses grew wildly, uncut, along with other vines and flowing bushes. There was a winding gravel path, so she followed it.

She came to a small gate set flush with the wall. Undoing the catch, she slipped out onto a sidewalk.

A glance up and down the street gave her her bearings; to her left and several blocks away, as she remembered, there were a number of shops. She'd be able to catch up a lift there, either a transit platform or a hitched ride.

Now, she told herself, she was a good little burber, out for a walk. She kept a quick pace. The feet would have no reason to stop her, she told herself. One block, then two. She risked a glance over her shoulder, found the sky empty of cars.

She came to the first of the shops. Since it was a Wednesday, things were slow. A few placid men and women wandered up and down the sidewalk, shopping, or going back to their parked aircars. She mixed among them. Only then did she begin to relax and breathe a bit easier. Her stride lengthened; she began to smile.

Ahead, a blond young man was carrying several small pressboard boxes. At a sleek little aircar he opened the luggage compartment and began stacking them inside. Shelly paused for a second, studying him, his short-cropped hair, his fashionable daysuit. He was just what she needed.

She walked up to him. "Excuse me," she said in a timid voice.

"Eh?" He looked at her, eyes widening a bit at the amount of cleavage her orange dress showed. She took a deep breath and his eyes widened further. It was then that she knew she had him hooked.

"My aircar just broke down," she said, "and I have a very pressing appointment centerSprawl. Might you possibly give me a ride to the nearest turbostation?"

"Sure," he said. "Don't mind at all. Always glad to give a lady a lift."

"Thank you," she said. "My name is Shelly Tracer."

"Bob. Bob Weinberg." He shook the hand she offered, then palmed the lock and held the passenger door open for her.

She smiled as she sat. "Thanks, Bob. I really appreciate this."

"No problem," he said. He went around and let himself into the driver's seat. "There's a big nexus just a couple of dozen kilometers ahead, if that's all right. You'll be able to catch a platform almost anywhere from there. Or perhaps I could drop you somewhere?"

"Oh, no, I don't want to take you out of your way—"

But he was already programming the autopilot. "Where to?"

"Broad III and Lexington, please."

"Okay. Be there in an hour."

She smiled her appreciation. It was so easy, she thought, to manipulate burbers. They were so predictable.

The aircar took off, repeller fields whirring with power. In seconds they were dozens of meters off the ground; the buildings dwindled to dollhouse-size as they found a place in the traffic flow and headed south at two hundred kay per hour.

As Shelly settled back and Bob prepared to make his oh-so-predictable play for a quick roll, a shadow crossed the window. Shelly glanced out.

It was a feet aircar, and the feet driver was motioning for them to land. A second later his partner sent a flare across the front of their windshield.

Bob cursed, then apologized. "Just what I need," he grumbled, "a ticket." He nosed the aircar toward the ground.

"You didn't do anything," Shelly said. "Don't worry about it."

"They'll find something. That's the problem with police. They're always around when you don't need them, never around when you do."

They coasted down to a clear street. Still grumbling, Bob shut off the repeller fields and let his aircar settle to a stop.

The feet aircar circled and landed in front of them, perpendicular to their aircar. The four feet inside went out the other side, weapons drawn, taking up positions to fire. Bob went dead-skin pale, and Shelly wasn't feeling too hot herself.

"Come out of the aircar with your hands raised," one of the feet shouted through a megaphone. "Any violent movements will be met with appropriate force."

"Shit," Bob whispered. "What did I *do?*"

He opened his door ever so slowly and eased out. Shelly followed. Outside, she kept her hands raised as high as she could.

The feet closed in. When three of them went for her, and only one for Bob, she knew without a doubt that she was their target.

Their leader slapped her up against the side of the aircar and searched her with impassionate thoroughness.

"She's not armed," he said, sounding a bit surprised.

"Of course not," Shelly said, again playing the defenseless woman. "Why would I be armed?"

"You're Shelly Tracer?"

"No."

That made him pause. She turned around and looked him in the eye. "Is there something I should know? What's this all about? And can I put my arms down now?"

He took a step back, looking less certain.

"She told me her name was Shelly Tracer!" Bob called from the other side of the aircar. "I didn't do anything, honest! I was just giving her a lift!"

Shelly gave him a sour look. "Thanks, Bob."

The feet's pistol had snapped up to cover her. There was a lopsided grin on his face. "Yeah. Had me going there for a moment, Tracer. But we got you, boy we got you!"

"So." Shelly spat to the side. "You've got me. What now?"

He took a pair of handcuffs from his belt, and while the other two feet covered her, he clipped them onto her wrists. He was none too gentle as he pulled her toward the feet aircar.

Remembering Karl, remembering what they'd done to his face, Shelly didn't put up a fight. Not here, not yet, she thought. There would be better chances later. First she had to put them off guard.

It was a long trip, and the feet were mainly concerned with patting themselves on the back for capturing her.

"Four feet capturing an unarmed woman," Shelly said, a touch of a sneer in her voice. "Very brave."

The one who'd put the handcuffs on her turned and grinned. "Lady, you're so hot you're up on SecurNet as top priority. It's been that way for a month. For you to stay out of sight that long, you've got to be a pro. You even lie like one. Don't give me that innocent look! I know the truth!" At that, he laughed.

Shelly settled back, looking out the window, watching the endless sea of concrete and brick buildings flow away below them. Strangely, she just felt tired and resigned, not angry as she'd always expected she'd feel if she got caught. She let out a long breath. She'd have a long rest now, the longest in her life. At least they hadn't caught her with any illegal hardware; the most she could get, she figured, would be twenty years in one of the colonial labor camps.

If you must win no matter what, cheat.

—Shelly Tracer
Theorems

—13—

AN hour later they landed in the northern end of the
Sprawl, in front of a row of bleak, graffiti-covered
warehouses. It wasn't the government detention
block she'd expected, or even an interrogation center; it
was just—*warehouses*. The place looked long abandoned.
Garbage littered the street, windblown paper, shards of
broken glass that caught the sun and gleamed like gems,
and even several burnt-out hulks of aircars, rust spreading
across the cracked pavement around them like orange
blood stains.

They dragged her from the aircar. Because it wasn't
what she'd expected, Shelly found herself acutely afraid.

She'd heard rumors of places that never existed officially, places whose existence was denied by every level of
government, placcs where prisoners could be tortured for
information, then mindwiped—or killed, if they were

lucky. She had a feeling this was one such unofficial interrogation center. A wave of sick despair washed through
her. If she'd had a gun, she would have blown her brains
out in that second.

When she tried to pull back, one of the feet rounded on
her, pulling her cuffed wrists up behind her back so white-
hot needles of pain shot through her shoulders.

"Walk or we'll club you down and carry you," he
snarled.

Shelly bit her lip hard. The pain and taste of blood
helped clear her mind. She obeyed, making an effort to
appear utterly defeated. With her hands cuffed behind her
back, they had her cold, she knew. And from the feet's
tone this wasn't bluster; he was nervous, edged, definitely
out of depth here. That could make him all the more dangerous if provoked. And she didn't want to provoke him:
he might kill when he only meant to hurt. As Johnny
would've said, as long as she was alive she had a chance.
It wasn't much of a hope, but it was all she had. She held
to it like a lifeline.

As they approached the nearest warehouse, a metal door
in its center rolled up, revealing a dark opening. Shelly
could see figures moving in the dimness. Finally a man in
a black SecurNet uniform appeared. He leaned up against
the doorway, arms crossed, smiling as though amused.

"Here she is," the first feet said. He didn't let go of
Shelly's arm.

"Yeah," said the second.

The SecurNet man showed a lot of perfect white teeth,
then nodded. He stepped forward and hooked Shelley's
arm, pulled her toward him. His hand was strong and very
warm. Shelly stared at his smooth, unlined face, the perfection of his eyes, and knew him to be modified, a metaman like herself, probably with steel bones and jumpwired
nerves. The two feet, though, didn't seem to know what

they were dealing with. The first one, the one who'd threatened Shelly, set his feet and kept hold of Shelly's other arm.

"Let's see some paperwork," he said. "We want our bonuses confirmed."

"They've already been taken care of." His voice held a trace of an accent, one which Shelly couldn't quite place. European? She didn't know.

"What?" The feet's eyes narrowed. "How?"

"One of our operatives has already confirmed Ms. Tracer's capture. Your pay bonuses have been entered; go back to your aircar and call your bank accounts for verification, if you wish."

"Yeah, we'll do that. And it better be square, or we'll take her with us."

The SecurNet man smiled. "Of course. We're always eager to cooperate with our police brethren." He held out his left hand. "The key to her handcuffs, please."

Silently, the feet passed them over. "Come on, Jon," he said, and he turned and stumped back toward the aircar.

"Inside, please, Ms. Tracer," the SecurNet man said, "and quickly. It's for the best, I assure you."

She went in. He followed, keying in a series of numbers on the lock. As the thick Durasteel door rolled down, Shelly took a moment for a quick glance around.

The warehouse had been partitioned off into at least two different segments; they were in the largest room, which was roughly a hundred meters long and twice that wide. Overhead, a latticework of steel girders supported the roof; the floor underfoot was plain concrete. Tables stood in long rows, and people sat at them working with electronic equipment, either assembling things or taking them apart; Shelly couldn't be quite sure which. In any case, it certainly didn't have the look of the medieval torture chamber she'd been expecting.

She turned questioningly to the SecurNet guard, but he wasn't paying any attention, seemed to be listening for something. A moment later there came a muted *bang* from outside, and she could feel the cement underfoot vibrate ever so slightly. The SecurNet man laughed and relaxed.

"What was that?" Shelly demanded.

"Explosions happen all the time around here. Pay no attention to them."

"The feet—?"

His smile became a wolfish grin. His teeth were too, too perfect. "There are too many of them, anyway; nobody will miss those few. Besides, Mr. Zedowski did not want word of your apprehension to get out. The fewer people who know, the fewer people who have to be silenced, correct?" Chuckling a bit, he inserted the key into her cuffs, released her, then stood patiently while she massaged her wrists. "Now," he said after a moment, taking her elbow and pulling her forward, "you're expected for a business conference." His tone left no room for dispute.

Shelly was herself a practiced killer, but she always felt something at another person's death. The offhand way the SecurNet man had killed those four feet made her realize yet again how alien his kind was. It only renewed her hatred and fear of Congress's private army.

That he'd uncuffed her meant he had no concern about her trying to escape. He was another metaman, after all, and she could easily imagine his body augmented until he was practically a one-man army. Chances were, she had nothing to match. Yes, she thought, she certainly wouldn't chance a break with him around.

And, she had to admit, the place aroused her curiosity more than a bit. Perhaps Johnny hadn't thrown her to the dogs, hadn't turned her over in the Disruptionist roundup. It was a small enough favor, considering all she'd done for him, all she'd tolerated. If the SecurNet guard *was* taking her to a conference with Johnny, all well and good. She had a few choice things she'd say—and do—to him, given half a chance. . . .

They entered a narrow hallway and stopped in front of another steel door. The man rapped twice, and while a buzzer sounded, he opened the door by its old-fashioned knob.

Johnny sat inside, at a desk, surrounded by equipment as illegal as any she'd ever seen before: his collection of slamjams and clockers seemed to have grown tremendously in the last month. Of course, with him heading SecurNet for Congress he could possess it all legally, and she knew he would've spared no expense in equipping himself. He was, after all, used to the best.

The SecurNet man pulled the door shut, leaving them alone.

Johnny laughed. "Shel, my dear! I'm so glad you could come."

"You bastard," Shelly said, advancing on him. As she said it, she had an odd feeling of déjà vu, as though they'd been through this all before. Only this time it was different, she told herself. This time he'd gone too far. This time she was going to kill him.

"I almost didn't recognize you. Orange really isn't your color."

"Bastard!"

"You're repeating yourself," he said. "Sit down."

"No."

"Shelly, Shelly, when are you going to learn to trust me? Everything I do is for the best. Now sit down or I'll have David come back and help you."

That was enough to make her think twice. Cursing to herself, Shelly moved toward the chair. Perhaps it would be best to wait, she decided suddenly. She could play it cagey, just as subtly as Johnny Zed ever did. She'd wait till she had him alone, had a chance to escape after killing him. That was the best idea.

She sat. When she did, restraints whipped around her arms and legs, binding her down more tightly than rope. She struggled against them briefly, more as a token gesture than anything else—a fight was expected—then abruptly sat back and glared at her captor.

Johnny had risen and come out from around his desk. Now she could see the mark of Congress upon him: the gold pentagons on his sleeves, the plushness of his black shirt and pants. He even seemed to have put on a bit of weight. It would have been easy for anyone to give in to Congress's lures, she thought. She'd almost given in herself to Lee Jones. But Johnny . . . she'd thought he'd be stronger.

"Come," he said to the chair, and, whirring, it rose on its own small repeller fields. When he opened the door it followed him into the hallway.

"Wait here for me," Johnny said to David, who was standing outside.

"Yes, sir," the metaman said.

Johnny walked down the hallway to a steel door like the one through which Shelly had entered. He keyed in a security code and palmed it, then the door rolled up. When he walked outside, the chair followed with Shelly.

This side of the building led into a small park that had run wild. Grass and weeds stood waist high; rows of hedges had become flowform lines of green. Even the trees seemed unkempt, their dead branches untrimmed, leaves piled deep around their twisted old trunks.

"It's safe here," Johnny said.

"Safe?" Shelly demanded.

"My office is bugged; we couldn't talk freely inside."

She spat. "Why would they bug you? You're their pet now."

"Oh, I wish they thought so, too! But none in Congress really trusts me, Shel, though they've given me a relatively important job. Karl insisted on it; they had to reward me for all my posturing as the man who destroyed the Disruption. As you know, we made sure the NewsNets got hold of the story and ran it into every home before it could be suppressed, making me a national hero. They had no choice but to pretend to like what I'd done, pretend to reward me. But my job is mostly a sham; I wield no real power here. It's all a device to get me out of the way so I don't cause any more trouble."

"That's supposed to change things? You're still a traitor!"

"Hardly that. The Disruption was already dead."

"Lies!"

"*Listen* to me, Shel!" He leaned forward until their faces almost touched, leaned forward until those deep blue eyes of his were peering deep into hers. Slowly, painstakingly, he said: "Nobody in Congress wanted the Disruption destroyed. Shelly, have you ever wondered why the Disruption never really struck any important blows in its fight against Congress? I'll tell you why. Because most of the Disruption's members were congressional spies."

His words fell like blows. "I don't believe that," Shelly said. But she heard the truth in his voice.

"How many important missions did we get sent on? *None*. Just minor annoyances that could easily be set right again. How many congressmen did we kill? *None*. What did we accomplish? *Nothing*. The Disruption was a tool of Congress. Look at things as they really are. Face the facts."

She didn't say anything, just stared at him, her mind numb. It seemed so impossible.

Johnny said, "Look at it this way: there are radicals in every society, people who want to change things for the better. Any sweeping reforms will alter the status quo—look at the Russian or Chinese revolutions, if you want examples. If you're in control of a country, like Congress is, you want to stay in control. So somewhere along the way someone got a bright idea: eliminate the radicals by controlling them. That's what the Disruption was, a way to control radicals like us. We were happy fighting against Congress; Congress was happy making sure we couldn't hurt them. It was a vicious circle. The only way to move on and actually accomplish something was to break free of the Disruption. Now that we've done that, we can get on with the fight, with the revolution."

"Why should I believe you?"

"Have I ever lied to you?"

"Yes, damn it!"

"When it mattered, I mean."

"What makes you think I even want to help?"

"I know you, Shel. You'll help."

She struggled against the chair's restraints. "Let me out of this damn thing!"

"Release," he said to the chair, and it let her go.

Standing, she stretched cramped muscles while she tried to sort out all her thoughts. On one hand she knew she'd been used. On the other, Johnny had a purpose, and she felt deep inside that he was right. On the third hand . . . on the third hand she was sick of him not bothering to tell her what was going on. Rescuing Karl, betraying the Disruption . . . he should have told her!

She turned to him, smiling, keeping every movement slow, easy, flowing. He was relaxed, looking off at the distant trees. Trusting, ever so trusting Johnny Zed. He knew she would never hurt him.

She hit him in the jaw as hard as she could. He never saw it coming.

He sprawled back on the grass, a dazed look on his face. After a minute he shook his head and tried to sit up.

"Damn," he said, gingerly touching his cheek. He spat a mouthful of blood. "Damn."

"Is there anything else you want to tell me?" Shelly said. She was trying to ignore the ache in her hand.

"Are you really prepared for the truth?" he asked.

"Yes."

"I mean the whole truth, bar nothing? It isn't always the best thing to know the truth about your friends."

"I think you owe it to me."

He patted the grass beside him. "Sit down, thcn. This is going to take a while."

As she sat, he leaned back and closed his eyes. Finally he began.

"I was Gilford or, rather, one of Gilford in the early days of the Disruption. No, don't interrupt. I'll explain it all as we go along. I was young then, idealistic, full of fire and anger to change things. That was when the Disruption was really alive, really *doing* things, before we were infiltrated and subverted.

"At that time we wanted a leader who would drive Se-curNet crazy when they tried to trace him down. So like the Luddites we invented one, Joseph S.L. Gilford, a philosopher, a revolutionary, a man of the world. I wrote his first two books of essays while others worked on spreading rumors about him. It was astonishing how many people wanted an underground revolutionary they could look up to. Americans have always rooted for the underdog, and Gilford seemed to catch the public fancy.

"But then my friends started disappearing one by one. They were replaced, of course—an organization as large as the Disruption needed a bureaucracy to run it. And the replacements were congressional plants, spies. When my turn came up to 'disappear,' I got lucky and managed to escape.

"I had a lot of friends in certain technical circles. They set me up with a new face and identity. I dropped out of sight for a few years.

"During that time Gilford's works were, I guess, written by congressional propaganda hacks. They were shrill, almost psychopathic tirades against the government rather than the pointedly philosophical works I wrote. That managed to put off much of the popular support Gilford had. And, without the people behind him, the Disruption could never succeed.

"It probably would have collapsed under its own weight at this point if Congess hadn't pushed to keep it going. It kept recruiting new members—the radicals and dissenters who would have made trouble on their own—and it channeled their energies in harmless directions.

"I was hurt and bitter for a while. Then I decided I still wanted to change things, so I decided to join the Disruption again, this time to destroy it. That's what I've been heading toward ever since we met, Shelly."

There was a cold numbness in her stomach. She believed him, believed him utterly. His story was so fantastic nobody, not even Johnny, could've made it up. *Gilford never existed. The Disruption was a sham.*

"What now?" she whispered.

"I protected you and Karl from the purge; you two were the only ones I trusted. Besides us, I have other friends willing to give support."

"What kind?"

"Technical. They're bright boys, on the cutting edge of just about every tech science you can think of. Whatever we need they can get—or do—if it involves information. I think that's the key to destroying Congress."

"No more bombs?"

"No more violence at all."

Shelly was nodding. "Where do I fit in?"

"I'm being watched too closely at the moment. You'll be my link to the rest of our little band. . . . Nexus, we're calling it. Are you with us?" There was a gleam in his eye, a feverish intensity, a drive and a power she could not resist.

"Yes!" she said.

He told her an address on St. Jude Street. "There's a turbostation five blocks west of here," he said, pointing. "Tell them you're there for Nexus. I've told them you're coming. They'll remember, get you set up."

Without another word he rose and walked back toward the warehouse.

Information is the key to the world.

—John Zedowski
Open Books

—14—

ST. Jude Street hadn't changed. Glitterfolk still walked among streeters and burbers, laughing, toying. Residue from a dozen different stimulant mists gave the air a bittersweet smell. Fiberoptics seemed the rule of the day; hair gleamed with streamers of colored sparks, and in places the blaze of light seemed brighter than the sun itself.

This time Shelly knew enough to avoid the skyeye bar. She entered St. Jude Street from the other direction, heading toward Animen-R-Us, watching as the numbers on the doors went steadily downward.

Finally she came to the correct address. It was the black door belonging to the techs, the same place she'd tried to hock Johnny's equipment what seemed a lifetime ago. Somehow, she wasn't surprised. Johnny'd said his friends were techs, after all, so it made a certain amount of sense. Drawing a deep breath, she stepped up.

The scanners whirred faintly. "What?" the speaker asked before she could ring the bell.

"I'm here for Nexus. Johnny sent me."

The door buzzed; she pushed it open and went in. A tall, rather emaciated-looking man greeted her this time. His short hair was flame red; he looked very young, definitely under twenty, Shelly thought. His glasses were dark in spite of the hallway's dim light.

"Welcome," he said. "You must be Shelly Tracer."

"Yeah. I'm surprised you recognize me."

"Johnny faxed us your pix four weeks ago. Your facial bone structure is . . . most distinctive. Also, you are the only one we were expecting for Nexus, so it had to be you. We had begun to wonder if you would ever appear."

"Johnny didn't call ahead and tell you I was coming?"

"Hmm? Of course not. He said you would be here, so of course you came, even though it took four weeks."

"Confident bastard."

"We are not here to play dominance games; we are here to win. This way, please."

He led her down a long hallway, past a number of closed Durasteel doors. Shelly could hear the muted sounds of voices and machinery behind several, but she didn't ask about them; the less she knew about techs and their secret projects, the better off she'd be, she thought. Finally they reached a lift. When they were both inside, he pushed the bottom button and they started down.

"How long have you known Johnny?" Shelly asked.

"As long as I can remember. He is one of the grand old men, and he has always been around, as far as I can tell. By the bye, I am Rad Lad, the one ghosting Nexus. I understand you are to run liaison between Johnny and the team, to stand as figurehead before the plebs."

"Yeah. That's what Johnny said."

"Do you have any useful skills?"

She bristled at that. "Damn right. You need something blown up, I'm the one to—"

"No, no," he said hastily, raising his hands, "I did not mean violent things. I meant *skills*, cracking, hacking. Do you play the boxes?"

"No."

"Pity." He sounded a bit wistful. "Well, perhaps it is for the best. You will probably be better off in negotiations if you do not know too much about the whys and hows of Nexus services—correct? But that can wait until later . . . you should meet the others in our merry little band."

The elevator doors opened onto a room like a huge cylinder standing on end. Giant vidscreen monitors lined the wall; each showed a different stream of numbers or swirling colored patterns. The room kaleidoscoped dizzyingly, disorientingly, and Shelly quickly focused her eyes on the center of the room. There, on flowform couches, two more people in white robes like Rad Lad's seemed to be sleeping. Light from the monitors made their faces appear to flicker like candles. Two more people moved around the little walkway in front of the monitors, keying numbers into handpads they carried.

"This is she," Rad Lad called.

The two on the walkway turned toward her; their eyeballs were silver, reflecting bloated images of the vidscreens. Shelly found herself staring. The two seemed to catch her unease, since they drew dark glasses from their pockets and put them on. Only then did Shelly take in their shockingly white hair, their smooth, moon-pale skin.

"Lord Hathgar and Anne Bonny," Rad Lad said, "may I present Shelly Tracer."

They nodded to her. Shelly noticed the one on the right was a woman; she seemed almost sexless in her white robe.

"And," Rad Lad continued, "currently jacked into the

system are Mask and Liberator. They are out of it; you can talk to them later, when they are downtime."

"Fine with me." Shelly walked to the left, looking at the monitors more carefully. She recognized only a little of what was on them: price updates from the stock market, NewsNet datafeeds, transmissions from satellites. "Is all this part of Nexus?" she asked.

Rad Lad followed her. "Yes. I assumed you knew all?"

"Johnny doesn't believe in telling anybody anything until he absolutely has to."

"Hmm. Well, you absolutely have to know what is going on here if you are to operate efficiently with us, so . . . I shall begin. Nexus Information Services is a data storage and retrieval company, at least on paper. This is the operating center, where incoming information is sorted, analyzed, stored, retrieved, and/or transmitted. We have the facilities to service up to thirteen thousand individual accounts. Your job will be to get those accounts for us."

"Sure," she said sarcastically, "and how am I supposed to do that?"

"Simple: as part of an incentive plan to win new accounts, three months of Nexus service will be offered for free to anyone who will accept it. The object is to take in as much private information on Congress and its members as we possibly can. Through that information will come various levers into power."

"Blackmail, you mean," Shelly said. "Isn't that it?"

"If you wish to be crude."

She laughed. "At least that's something I can understand. And if it's blackmailing Congress, I'm all for it! But how am I going to get thirteen thousand accounts? That'll take years!"

He smiled as he shook his head. "Thirteen thousand is the theoretical maximum number of individuals we can handle with only two people jacked into the system at one

time. Since there are only six hundred and fifty-four senators and representatives, and since ten percent of that
number would do as an adequate sample, it should not be
too hard."

"Only sixty-five . . ."

"More would be better. Consider sixty-five the minimum."

"It sounds possible."

"Indeed," he said. "We have an office prepared for you.
I will take you to it. This way, please?"

He led her back into the lift and brought her up one more
floor. When the doors opened, Rad Lad glanced at the opticon controls and the hallway flooded with light.

"Your office is at the end of this hallway," he said,
pointing. "Everything you need should be there. I will let
you settle in; I have a number of other commitments that
require my immediate attention. Should you need anything, ask and it will be provided."

When Shelly stepped out, the lift's doors closed. She
paused, listening, but didn't hear anything; the place had a
desolate feel, as though nobody had been here in weeks, if
not months. The air tasted dry, stale, recycled.

Best get on with it, she told herself. She went to the door
Rad Lad had indicated. The handpad hadn't been initial-
ized, so she stored her print there and went in.

The place had been simply yet elegantly furnished. The
realwood desk, plush red carpet, and pale blue wallpaper
spoke of both wealth and good taste. Etchings of camels
and lions and other extinct animals decorated the walls.
Directly behind the desk was a panoramic view of the
Sprawl as seen from the upper floor of a skyscraper. As
Shelly watched, a flock of pigeons winged past; the picture
was a simuscreen, designed to make the place look like an
upper-floor office to anyone she spoke to on the vidphone.

Smiling, she sat down at the desk, leaned back in the

seat. It was immensely comfortable. Stacks of papers lay before her, and she leafed through them idly, finding detailed lists of the services Nexus offered. Too, there was a long list of congressmen's private vidphone numbers. Johnny hadn't missed a thing.

She spent the rest of the afternoon reading about Nexus and its operations. On the surface it looked like another of the myriad data storage and retrieval services, only with quite a few little hitech extras tucked in, such as access to any of the NewsNet channels and various library information banks.

Fascinated by all that Nexus could do, Shelly lost track of time. When next she looked up, Rad Lad was standing in the doorway, smiling a bit. He walked in, white robes rustling.

"Absorbed in your work, I see," he said.

"I want to do a good job."

"Of course. It is getting late, though, and I thought you might wish to be shown your quarters."

She rose and restacked the papers on the desk. "I suppose the rest can wait."

Two days later, with all the information she needed memorized or lying close at hand for reference, Shelly was ready to get started. Her hair had been dyed back to its normal color, her orange-tinted skin bleached, her teeth whitened: no trace of her makeover remained. She liked it that way.

First on her list to contact was the Speaker of the House, Lee Jones. She punched his number into the vidphone and waited while it dialed. A moment later a young woman with spiked green hair smiled back from the screen. Shelly recognized her as one of the glitterfolk from Lee's private party.

The woman said, "Lymington Jones's office, Cathy speaking. May I help you?"

"Yes, please. Is Lee in?"

"One moment, please, Ms. Tracer." The screen went dark and soft, soothing music played.

She remembered me, Shelly thought. That was a good sign; she must have made a favorable impression.

A moment later the Speaker of the House picked up the call. His office looked large, elegant from what little Shelly could see of it.

"Shelly!" Lee said. "Wonderful, simply wonderful to hear from you! I tried to reach you last week at the senator's house but couldn't get through. Nothing serious, I hope."

"No, not at all. I was out of town on business."

"Well, what can I do for you? I trust you've reconsidered my offer of a job, then?"

Shelly laughed. "No, I'm afraid not, Lee. I've taken a position with Nexus Information Services. I'm afraid I've left politics for good. As a matter of fact, I'm calling on Nexus business."

"Okay. What's up?"

"I'd like to offer you our services."

He shrugged a bit apologetically. "I'm afraid I already use Data House."

"Data House is little more than a filing cabinet. Nexus offers everything Data House does—with the same complete confidentiality, of course—along with fifteen other services."

"Such as?"

"Access to all public and subscription datafeeds as part of our monthly fee. Any of several thousand topics and subtopics can be flagged; when bulletins relating to them come across the feeds, they will be automatically routed to your terminal. There are also online mail services, bulletin boards, shopping and investment services, and complete financial services to any NetBank in the world."

She saw his facial muscles relax into impassivity; he was trying to hide his interest. "It seems like something I might be able to use," he admitted. "What's the cost?"

"Twelve thousand per month. The first three months of online service are being offered free as an introductory premium."

"Do you have literature?"

"Of course."

"Fax it to me. I'll look it over and get back to you tomorrow."

"Right away."

"Another question. Is Senator Winston using Nexus?"

She smiled confidentially. "I'm sorry, but the names of our clients must remain confidential. I can say that a number of prominent members of Congress are already using Nexus, though, and we've heard nothing but praise from them."

"I'll look into it further."

"Certainly. I'll fax you our brochure. I'm sure you'll agree Nexus is the best information service around. Talk to you later, Lee."

"Bye."

Shelly smiled. From the look on Lee's face, she knew she had him hooked.

She keyed in the next congressman's number. With Representative Jones and Senator Winston as subscribers, she knew the rest of Congress would beat a path to Nexus's door. Nobody wants to be left out—congressmen least of all.

The next few weeks seemed to pass with an almost blinding speed. Lee Jones signed on, as did close to a hundred others. Inquiries were stacking up in Shelly's office faster than she could answer them—and not just from congressmen. Word of mouth about Nexus seemed to have made it one of the hottest services around. Shelly found herself talking to judges, career bureaucrats, businessmen . . . all the associates, hangers-on, and friends of Lee Jones and his ilk. Every morning brought more calls than the previous one, and Shelly found herself staying longer and longer each night to try to catch up.

Finally she had to admit defeat. "The work is getting out of hand," she told Rad Lad. "I'm going to need help."

"What kind?"

"A private secretary to take care of all the routine correspondence."

"I'll see what I can do," he said.

The next morning a bald man in white robes and dark glasses was waiting for Shelly outside her office. Beside him stood a large cart covered by a sheet.

"I am Lolo," he said simply.

"Shelly. You're here to help with Nexus?"

He nodded.

"Good." She let him in.

At once Lolo wheeled his cart to the side wall. He removed the cover, revealing a monitor and some rather large silver boxes that hummed ever so faintly. He jacked the boxes into datafeed outlets in the wall, then dragged a reclining chair over from in front of Shelly's desk. Leaning back, he seemed to relax.

Only then did he remove his sunglasses. His eyes were completely silver. As he stared at the monitor, information began to scroll across its screen. Shelly watched over his shoulder, waiting for questions, as he went through all the replies she'd made to requests for information on Nexus. He was probably analyzing her style of writing, she thought. She waited, but he didn't ask any questions.

Finally he stopped reviewing old records. Letters requesting information about Nexus began flashing across the screen at the rate of several per minute, and he answered them just as fast.

Shelly just sighed and went to her desk, feeling obsolete. If Johnny hadn't needed a real person for a front, someone Congress could check on, she thought the metamen could have taken care of everything in a tenth the time. She regarded Lolo over the top of her vidphone. He didn't quite seem *human*, somehow . . . more a robot, or a puppet. If only he made some noise as he worked, or moved around a little bit instead of lying there like a braindead corpse.

At least she had one consolation: she knew that nobody would sign up to a dataservice being hawked by someone like him. That made her smile. Yes, the techs needed her, just as she needed them to get back at Congress for all it had done to her country. They made a perfect team.

She glanced over her correspondence. She still had dozens of calls to return, and almost a hundred followup offers to make to hesitant congressmen. It looked like a busy day indeed.

Things began to settle into an easier routine toward her ninth week of working with Nexus. Every day Rad Lad came to see her at lunch, dinner, and quitting time. If it weren't for him, Shelly thought, she would have missed half her meals and fallen asleep at her terminal every night. She saw Johnny only once, when he stopped in to drop off copies of the governmental budget and tax reports. He didn't have time to stay; he had meetings to attend.

In the tenth week Rad Lad showed up well before lunchtime. Since Shelly had him pegged as a man of routine, she knew something had happened. She keyed away her letter and stood.

"Johnny is here," Rad Lad said. "He has called a conference."

"I'd been wondering what he's up to."

He shrugged. "Johnny has not said. It must be something important, however. We shall see."

He led her up two more floors, to a large steel door. Shelly waited impatiently while the various security mechanisms analyzed his handprint and retinal patterns. Finally the door folded aside.

They entered a cavernous, dimly lit room. There were flare lamps in the ceiling, but the walls seemed to absorb light. She couldn't hear her own footsteps, Shelly noticed, even though the floor felt like concrete.

In the center of the room was a round table. Johnny sat facing them. As always, he was impeccably dressed, once again in a black SecurNet uniform. Lord Hathgar and Mask sat to his right; to his left were Anne Bonny and Liberator. The techs all wore their usual white robes and dark glasses.

"Finally we are all together," Johnny said. His voice sounded too quiet, almost lost, as though something were muting it. He grinned as Shelly and Rad Lad took the two empty seats. "I'd been meaning to send you a memo, Shel. You're doing quite well in signing up congressmen, beyond our initial estimates."

She nodded. "Thanks. Now, what's all this about? Have you found anything yet?"

"Yes—or rather, Anne has. That's why I called the meeting. She's uncovered a slight discrepancy between what Congress levies in taxes and what it spends every year in its budget."

"I do not understand," Rad Lad said. "Everyone knows Congress works on a deficit."

"Do they, now?" Johnny's grin grew wider. "What would you say if I told you Congress takes in significantly more than it spends?"

"How much is gone?" Shelly said.

Johnny looked at Anne Bonny, eyebrows raised.

"Seven hundred an' forty-three *trillion* dollars, give or take th' odd billion," Anne said. Her voice sounded strained, as though she could scarcely believe it herself. "It's simply gone—vanished in number jugglin'."

Shelly leaned back, stunned to silence. That was more than the entire country's budget for the next two years. She looked at Johnny. "Who—" she began. "How long—"

"I'll let Anne answer that," Johnny said. "She's the one that's handled all the data."

Anne Bonny spread a printout across the table. "You all can see where th' problem begins—there, in '09. I figure it started with a surplus of funds after all departmental allocations were made. Rather'n hold the money f' next year, it simply vanished into Swiss accounts. I've got th' account numbers, an' I'm lookin' to identify th' owners. We ought t' have names in a few hours."

"Incredible," Rad Lad murmured.

"Is this what you wanted?" Shelly asked.

Johnny nodded grimly. "When the people find out, I can't see them holding still for it. Money is the one thing that they all—glitterfolk, burbers, and streeters alike—have in common. It's cost them literally thousands of dollars each to keep Congress in power." He grinned, but there was no humor or triumph in it, only a sick sort of sadness. "I think," he said, "we've found our lever."

Machiavelli said the ends justify the means. Of course he was wrong. When you believe in something strongly enough, you don't have to justify your actions to anyone.

—John Zedowski
New Papers

—15—

"**G**OT time for a walk?"

Shelly looked up, startled. Johnny stood in the doorway, dressed out as a burber in various shades of gray. He was grinning that jack-dumb grin of his, confident, sure of himself and knowing it.

"Yeah." She finished up her letter and mailed it, then tabbed off the keyboard and watched it fold into the desk. "Something's happening?"

"We have an audience with the senator."

"Karl?"

"Sandy, now, if you don't mind. Better get used to calling him that; it looks as though he'll be playing his father till the end of his life."

"Poor Karl."

"Sacrifices must be made. He knew what might happen

before he accepted the job, and he's prepared for it. And his name is Sandy now."

"Sandy, then," Shelly said. As they headed for the door she asked, "Nothing's upset the plan, has it?"

"Quite the contrary. I now have all the information I need. In fact, there's no reason for you to continue at Nexus . . . it's all but over."

Shelly had a million questions to ask but bit her lip and managed to hold them back. Johnny would tell her when he was good and ready, probably when they were all together in the aircar. A hallway wasn't the place; anyone might overhear. Besides, she thought, if Johnny wouldn't talk, there was always Karl; he'd never be able to keep a secret from her.

They took an elevator up to the rooftop landing pad, where Senator Winston's private aircar was waiting for them. As she stepped out into the bright sunlight, Shelly had to squint and shield her eyes with one hand. It seemed years since she'd been outside. The warm, humid air, the smell of hot tar and exhaust fumes and sweat and rotting garbage from the street, it all struck her at once in a wave. Sweat began to trickle down her back and sides.

As she hurried to the aircar, Johnny followed a step behind. The door hissed open for her and she climbed in, sliding into a seat at the table opposite Karl.

Karl nodded to her, tiny lines crinkling around his eyes and mouth, and again Shelly couldn't help but notice how tired and old he looked. Worries of Congress and Nexus and the new revolution must have aged him, she thought. But then he'd always been running the greatest risk: he had to be a different person *every* minute of the day—had to live, breathe, talk, and move like his father. One mistake could've exposed him for the imposter he was. Even though Esteban Grammatica had done a perfect job on his body, Karl's mind still had to be molded, retrained to his father's ways. The stress it caused showed.

"How's it, Shel?" he said. His voice was strong as ever, though, and it held a new crackle of authority . . . a senator's voice, she thought.

She said: "Johnny mentioned news. You got the names on the accounts, right?"

"Yeah." He watched Johnny seal the door. "Every one of them. There were few surprises."

Johnny pushed the intercom button and spoke in low tones to Lang, the chauffeur. A moment later the aircar's repellers roared, powering up, preparing for takeoff.

"So tell me!" Shelly said.

Johnny slid into the seat next to her, wiping his brow with his sleeve. "We have the names," he said. "Eighty-six in all."

She leaned forward, eager. "Who?"

Karl said, "Groves. Hallett. Ibatsu. Echevarria. Gosset. Baltadonis—the list goes on and on. All the greater congressional families are involved to some degree, including, I'm sad to say, my own."

"Yeah. I believe it. The bastards had to be sucking the country dry for years to be living the way they do."

"Then you wouldn't be surprised if I told you Lee Jones seems to be their leader?"

Shelly blinked. "What?"

"I told you he wasn't so nice as you thought," Johnny said. "He does his best to put on a charming front, but underneath he's one of the most ruthless men around. You *knew* that. Karl and I told you the first time you met him."

"I knew," Shelly said, her jaw tightening. It explained that estate of his, how he could afford so many parties with the glitterfolk. "I didn't want to believe it, but I knew. The bastard."

Karl said, "He's spent at least forty-seven trillion dollars in the last few years. Personally."

She gaped. "Nobody could spend that much!"

"He bought his estate two years ago for seventeen trillion dollars. He's been spending money that lavishly ever since he inherited the family seat. He lives better than a king. Oh, yes, Shelly, he spent that much money all right."

"Just so you haven't made a mistake. If he turned out to be innocent . . ."

"The accounts aren't in his name, of course," Johnny said. "That's why the trackdown took so long. The money's being held by consortiums of companies that don't exist, except on paper. We had to follow the money as it was withdrawn, through dummy accounts, through holding companies, through a tangle of blind alleys and hidden transfers. But finally we cracked their final level of security, and after that the names came pouring out."

"What's next?"

"This is what we've been waiting for," Johnny said. "This is the straw that will break Congress's back, change the world as we know it!"

Shelly couldn't help but sneer. "Sure it will, Johnny. Shit, man, they'll just laugh in your face if you confront them! Maybe—if they're feeling kind—they'll offer to buy you off. Most likely they'll just laugh, then have one of their gunmen kill you, head of SecurNet or no."

"You're a cynic, Shel. Congress isn't a single entity with one mind and one body. It might be dangerous if it were. Rather, it's made up of constantly squabbling factions that put on a facade of unity to deal with the outside world. More realistically, if we expose the thieves, a scandal and internal investigation will result. The guilty ones will bolt to Switzerland or Brazil and spend the rest of their lives there living high and happy off their bank accounts."

"So a few of them go. There are plenty of others to take their place."

"We've thought about that. Congressmen are essentially rabbits who bought off the foxes—creatures easily led. The senator here won't be implicated in the scandal in any way, and he's the only top official who won't be . . . so when a power vacuum opens up, when the others ditch Congress, he'll be in tight."

"I'll call for reforms," Karl said, "elections. A new president to make sure such thefts never happen again. The people will back me—"

Shelly paused, thinking. It almost seemed plausible the way they put it, yet something was niggling at the back of her mind. Suddenly she realized what it was.

"That still won't get the money back," she said.

"Losses are inevitable. And, of course, we'd get some of the money back by seizing the guilty congressmen's estates and property in the U.S."

"That couldn't be more than a few trillion!"

"It might be as much as a hundred trillion. It'll take months if not years to sort through all the records, but it can be done."

Shelly said, "That other six hundred trillion dollars would go a long way toward rebuilding the government. . . ."

Johnny shrugged. "Funds will be raised and allocated as necessary."

"How can you ask people to pay even higher taxes? The peasants always have to bear the cost of a revolution. It isn't fair, Johnny, and you know it!"

"Life isn't always fair. And the peasants are rich here; in the long run it would be better for them."

Shelly snorted. "Nobody's rich enough for that."

"Well, what do you suggest?" Karl said.

"Simple." Her words were hard, sharp. "Steal it back.

You're a tech, Johnny—Rad Lad says you're the best around. Just break into the congressmen's accounts and transfer it all to Nexus."

Johnny laughed. "It's not that easy, Shel, though I wish it were!"

"What's so hard? You know where the money is. You've been poking through their accounts for a month. What's to stop you from just taking it?"

"In case you hadn't noticed, there's a difference between *looking* at records and *changing* them—a big difference. There are all sorts of security measures I couldn't even begin to crack without the access codes. Even then it would be tricky, dangerous. Switzerland guards its money better than anyone else in the world, period."

"These codes, though. With them you could do it?"

"Probably," Karl said. "We've been through all this before, Shel."

"Definitely," Johnny said. "But we don't have them, and that's the end of that."

"Where would they be?" Shelly said.

"Locked away, probably in a safe."

"Where?"

"As I said, the largest withdrawals have all been by Lee Jones. He'd need the codes for that."

She pursed her lips. "Well, it must be done. We've got to get the money back."

"How?" Karl said.

"I'm going to get the codes," Shelly said. "No objections. I'll be in and out jack-quick, hit and run. The job's mine."

Johnny seemed to be smiling a bit, as though he'd expected it, as though he'd planned for her to steal the codes, but he said nothing more. Suddenly Shelly felt suspicious, used. She remembered the last time Johnny'd wanted her to do something like this, the time the feet had captured

Karl. Johnny'd tricked her then, lied to her, told her Karl was his brother. It had all worked out in the long run, but short time it had been enough of a mess to almost get her killed.

She had the distinct feeling he'd just tricked her into volunteering again. This time, though, she'd make sure she was prepared, make certain she had the right tools for the job. She had to look out for herself, after all.

"Yeah," she said slowly, "I'll go." She didn't like it, but she'd go. It was for the good of all—not just Johnny or Karl or the Disruption, but for all Americans. Her country came before them. It had always been that way with her, and she knew it always would be.

But sometimes Johnny made it so hard.

There is a difference between murdering a man and killing a man. Murder involves a deliberate act for personal vengeance. Killing is an act which has no personal feeling, as with an army fighting a war. There can be pointless killing. But it is still not murder.

—John Zedowski
Revolution Today

—16—

"YOU can't go in alone," Johnny said.

"I didn't think you'd let me."

He looked at her strangely for a second. Then he gave a little shrug and said, "I'm going with you. I can get you past most of Jones's security devices."

"Fine, I'd hoped you'd come. Before we do anything, I'll need time to get outfitted, and I imagine you have things to get for yourself."

"Rad Lad has everything you could possibly want in Tech House."

Shelly laughed. "Oh? I want a lot of special equipment. I won't go in this time unless I have it."

Smiling, he said, "Wait and see, then."

He spoke to Lang again on the intercom and the aircar descended rapidly, touching down on Tech House's rooftop pad. Johnny stood and opened the door for Shelly.

"Don't give me this shit," she said. A heartbeat later, more politely: "After *you*."

Grinning that jack-dumb grin of his, he stepped down. She followed, frowning. If anything, the day had gotten hotter, more humid; the sun was hazed in gray.

Karl called after them, "Good luck to you both!"

Shelly turned and waved. Luck they could certainly use, the more of it the better. Behind her the aircar's repeller fields began to whir loudly, powering up. Little grains of sand stung the back of her neck and hands. Then the aircar lifted, sending dust roiling in little clouds, and it was gone.

They reached the entranceway and Johnny palmed the handpad. In a moment the lift door opened; Rad Lad was inside, leaning against the far wall.

"Hmm?" he said.

"Tonight," Johnny said.

"You're too used to tricking people," Shelly said to Johnny, to them both. "All you had to do was ask me. I would've gone, and happily. Lee Jones deserves all the pain and aggravation we can give him. But you should have asked. I would've gone. Really, you should've asked."

Johnny didn't seem the slightest bit apologetic. "So it goes."

"Arrogant bastard."

"I love you, too, Shel."

Rad Lad said to her, "You must get your equipment. We should have everything you want here."

"Yeah, well, I want a lot of things—hand weapons, plastics . . . perhaps some gas grenades."

"I shall take you to the armory." Rad Lad punched one of the lower buttons; Johnny pushed another.

The armory, Shelly soon discovered, lay in yet another cavernous chamber far underground. The techs must have carved out rooms and tunnels beneath the streets for blocks in all directions, she thought; but then, they had the money and the power to do it. As she walked down the aisle past racks of handguns and rifles, crates packed with gas cannisters, boxes of ammo, hand rockets, grenades, and plastic explosives, she marveled at their ability to get so much equipment so secretly. She'd always thought of techs as nonviolent, too, and found the presence of the arsenal almost as disconcerting as its contents, if not more so. There were even a couple of small missile launchers pushed up against the far wall. As she moved through the rows of boxes, she studied the labels. Most, she found to her surprise, belonged to SecurNet.

"Do you approve of my selections?" Rad Lad asked. "I tried to be complete."

"Yeah, it's complete all right. There's enough here to outfit an army!"

"Johnny had me gather it in case open rebellion broke out. We would equip streeters for an assault on D.C."

"I'm sure SecurNet didn't cooperate!"

"But they did. They delivered everything to us."

"I'll bet!"

"Hmm? It is just a matter of requesting an arms drop to reinforce existing troops. They are eager to supply their people with more weapons. Only we were there to pick them up instead."

"There's got to be more than that. I've never heard of anyone else doing it!"

He inclined his head a fraction of a centimeter. "Perhaps there is a bit more than that, but I could only explain it properly in terms of access and instruction codes—the *how* of the weapon drops. Rather, let us proceed with equipping you. Is everything you need present?"

"Yes, and then some!" She found a crowbar and used it to open a crate of gas grenades, then began stacking a half-dozen of the little silver globes beside her. "I'll need a bag to carry what I take."

"I will get one."

Half an hour later Shelly had selected an impressive array of explosives, gas and frag grenades, pistols, and even a fully automatic combat rifle with laser sights. These she stowed away in the backpack Rad Lad provided. After tabbing it closed, she hefted it experimentally.

"Are you sure you should take so much?" Rad Lad asked. "It must weigh forty kilos."

With a grunt Shelly swung it over her shoulder. The weight was familiar, reassuring. "I've carried more than this before," she said. "And it's better to be prepared for anything. I can always ditch some of it if I need to run."

Shaking his head doubtfully, Rad Lad accompanied her back to the elevator. He looked at his watch. "Johnny will be on the roof by now," he said. "We obtained a two-seater aircar, without markings, as he requested."

"Thanks."

The lift arrived. After two techs with silver eyes got off, Shelly stepped in and punched the top button. She waited impatiently as the doors hissed shut.

Finally they opened again. It was late in the afternoon now, and the sky had become overcast; dark thunderheads were rolling in from the west. *Just what we need*, she thought bitterly. Perhaps it would help them, though: she'd once read that fewer crimes were committed during bad weather . . . thieves didn't like getting wet any more than normal folk, so they tended to work only on clear nights. That being the case, feet and SecurNet forces might well be off guard. But she still didn't look forward to the idea of lugging forty-odd kilos of weapons across Jones's estate.

There was a small black aircar parked there, as Rad Lad had said, and it had darkened windows. As she walked toward it, she noted that it had no identification marks other than the license tags . . . which were probably faked as well.

She circled to the passenger door and pulled it open. Sure enough, Johnny was sleeping inside, his seat tilted back as far as it would go. Shelly made no attempt to keep quiet as she stowed her pack in the luggage compartment, then slid beside him.

When she slammed her door shut, Johnny sat up and yawned.

"Ready?" he said.

Shelly nodded. "Yeah. For anything."

He activated the autopilot, which began powering up the repellers, and said, "It'll be dark by the time we get to Jones's estate. You might as well catch a quick nap. I certainly intend to."

Silently she settled back. She could feel the tension beginning to build within her, and she knew she wouldn't sleep no matter how she tried. But she also knew it would be a long night. It couldn't hurt, she thought, to rest a bit. So she settled back and closed her eyes, listening to the thrum of the repellers, the whisper of wind, and longed for the peaceful days to come.

They reached Jones's estate just as the sun was setting. The autopilot beeped insistently until Johnny took the controls himself.

Rubbing her eyes, Shelly looked out across the huge expanse of grass and trees. As she did, floodlights began clicking on one by one, casting stark shadows among the trees, lighting the lawns and flowerbeds as though it were day.

Johnny switched on the vidphone. In a moment he had one of the SecurNet guards in charge of Jones's estate on the line.

"I wish landing clearance," Johnny said.

"Identify yourself."

"Shelly Tracer and escort to see Representative Jones."

"Mr. Jones is unavailable at the moment."

"We'll wait."

"Clearance denied. Proceed no further; this is the only warning you will receive. If you wish to see Representative Jones, make an appointment with his secretary tomorrow during business hours."

The vidphone flickered with static, then went dark.

"That's that," Johnny said. He swung the aircar around and headed north, watching the dashboard.

Shelly knew him too well to think he was giving up: there had to be trackers monitoring them, she thought. When they were a safe distance away, he'd land and they'd make their way back on foot.

Sure enough, a few moments later Johnny set the aircar down in a small clearing. Now, Shelly knew, came the hard part: getting past the estate's guards and security devices.

She opened her door, grabbed her pack, and slid out. The air was stiflingly hot and humid; in the distance, thunder rumbled. She looked over to Johnny, but he was no more than a vague shadow beneath the trees.

"Ready?" she asked.

"Of course." He stepped closer and she could just make out a dark mask over his face. Something flickered like tiny red flames where his eyes should have been—probably lenses of some kind, altering the spectrum of light so he could see, Shelly decided.

"Let's go," Johnny said.

She led the way. There was a winding trail that headed toward Jones's house. They followed it single file, Shelly feeling her way along step by step, Johnny on her heels. Twice she found tripwires attached to flashblind grenades, and four times she found landmines geared to human weight, all of which they carefully avoided.

Finally the trees began to thin; illumination from the floodlight filtered through, grew brighter until Shelly could see her way clearly for the first time. Still she continued to feel her way along, inch by inch, searching for the traps she knew had to be there.

Three optical scanners later, they came to a two-meter-deep drainage ditch with smoothly sloping concrete sides; a trickle of water gleamed at its bottom. Shelly tossed a pebble into it, listening as it rattled along the concrete and splashed into a puddle. Johnny touched her arm as she moved forward.

"First alarm," he said. He gestured toward the other side of the ditch. "There are beams of light crisscrossing the surface. We shouldn't break them."

"Is there a clear way across?" Shelly said.

Johnny turned to the left, then to the right, scanning. "I don't see any. We might as well cross here. I can get us through, but it's going to take time. Sit down; relax."

Shelly shrugged off her pack and sat with her back against a tree. Carefully Johnny opened up his own pack. Spreading out a plastic sheet, he began to assemble a large device with numerous protruding arms.

Lightning flashed, nearer this time. Shelly counted two seconds before she heard the thunderclap. Then came a pitter-patter running sound from the leaves overhead. Looking up, she felt a few drops of rain against her cheek.

"Shit!" Johnny said. Quickly he disassembled his equipment and stuffed it back into the case, throwing the plastic sheet in on top.

"Afraid of a little water?" Shelly struggled to her feet.

"Damn rain would short my mimic out. We'll have to wait till it stops."

"Or till it's pouring. They'll think the rain is distorting the beams."

"Possibly."

"Undoubtedly."

He joined her next to the tree, turning up his collar. They didn't have to wait long: lightning flashing, thunder roaring, the rain pounded down harder and harder. At last it became a drenching torrent and the drainage ditch began to fill with runoff water.

"Ready?" Shelly called.

Johnny shouldered his pack and nodded.

Together they raced to the drainage ditch, slid down to the stream at its bottom, and splashed across. Somehow they managed to push and pull and scramble their way up to the other side in record time.

Johnny's eyes still glowed red behind his mask. He took Shelly's arm and guided her quickly down the path. Several times they left it for a few meters, but they always returned—skirting laser-triggered traps or alarms, Shelly thought.

Once she heard the whir of an aircar close by. They hunched down under the cover of a broad oak and waited till it passed.

"I hate rain," Johnny whispered, as it began to let up a bit.

"I love it," Shelly said. "It exhilarates me!"

"It kills electronics."

She laughed and pulled him up. "Lead on."

After another hundred meters the trees suddenly ended. Then the open expanse of lawn lay before them, with its hedges and flowerbeds, its little fishponds and gazebos. Floodlights shone brightly, creating misty globes of radiance in the rain.

"Well?" Shelly asked, as Johnny slowly turned to take it all in.

"There are power sources *there*, *there*, and *there*," he said, pointing. "Probably vidcameras. They'll be standard

SecurNet equipment, plain but serviceable. Keep your distance and they won't pick you up in weather like this."

As she started forward, he grabbed her arm and pulled her back to cover. "SecurNet patrol," he whispered in her ear.

"I'll take him down," she whispered back.

She strained to see. Slowly, too slowly, a man ambled toward them, shoulders hunched forward. He had a flashlight in one hand and a rifle slung over his shoulder; his cap was pulled down so the brim protected his eyes from the rain. He seemed more intent on finishing his rounds than watching for prowlers, and somehow, on a night like this, Shelly didn't blame him.

From her pack she took a length of strong wire, which she wound around her hands into a strangler's garrote. As the guard passed, he didn't give a glance in their direction.

Shelly crept onto the grass, shadowing him, silent as a spider. When she got close enough, she looped the wire around his neck and snapped it tight, kicking his legs out from under him. He fell, clutching at her wrists, and she fell on top of him, knees on his shoulders. She twisted the line, tightening it. The man's eyes bulged. Finally he gave a little shudder and lay still.

Johnny ran out and helped her drag the corpse back to cover. Beneath the trees they went through the man's pockets, finding little of use outside of his SecurNet card; but then, Shelly thought, Johnny could get them through any door it would open. Of more interest was his equipment. The rifle was standard SecurNet issue, loaded with twenty rounds of plastic fléchettes, and the knife sheathed in his boot was serrated on both sides of the blade, fighting style. There were six notches in its handle: people he'd killed during riots, Shelly knew. That was yet another reason SecurNet disgusted her.

"You're about his size," Johnny said. "Put on his uniform."

Shelly thought about it for a half-second, then nodded. It was probably a good idea, in case one of the vids spotted her. She could move pretty freely across the grounds that way.

They stripped the corpse quickly. Johnny helped her put on the shirt and pants, which were a bit loose, but it was dark and with her belt tightened, she didn't think anyone would notice. She shrugged on her backpack; since it was black, nobody would notice it. Then, pulling the cap down over eyes, she started from cover.

"Wait." He took a small, round clasp from his pocket and clipped it to her shirt collar. "Microphone. That'll keep us in touch."

"Great." Casually swinging the SecurNet rifle, Shelly moved out to the lawn and continued along the path, studying the house as she went. It was exactly as she remembered: it sprawled across hundreds of meters, huge, rambling, three stories high. The lawn completely encircled it; they couldn't possibly sneak up. What she had to do, she decided, was take out the SecurNet men monitoring the vidcameras.

She said so to Johnny.

The little microphone hissed for a second. "Probably not possible," he said at last. "They're bound to be inside the house, not out on the grounds. If you could get to them, it would be just as easy to get to Jones's study. And the fewer guards we meet, the safer we'll be."

"Coward," she said.

"Realist," he said, just as quickly. "Heroics are for heroes. Let's just get the job done."

"I thought you fancied yourself a hero."

"It's hard, when you're standing under a tree, shivering and soaking wet. Just get me in safely?"

"Sure, Johnny. No problem."

She turned down a sidewalk, heading for a door set deep in shadows as though it were part of her job to check it. Nobody challenged her authority. Yet.

This is too easy, she thought.

Then she saw the opticon set in the wall to the door's right. She stared at it a full thirty seconds—a thousand times longer than it needed to scan her retinal patterns and decide whether it wanted to let her it. She couldn't possibly get through it, short of burning it out with a laser.

"There's an opticon lock," she whispered to Johnny, "on the side door."

"I can deal with it, if I have to. But the house might have electronic probe sensors implanted. Can you get someplace high up, so you can look for another way in?"

"I think so."

"Good. I've charted the vidcameras' positions, and I should be able to follow you to the house without being seen."

"Okay. Wait." She eased herself behind the bushes to the door's right. The wall was made of stones set in a random pattern, some jutting out from the others as much as ten centimeters.

She began to climb. Her toes hurt and her Korean fingers ached from holding her weight, but at last she hauled herself up onto rain-slick tiles. This roof was designed to channel water from two large drains; that seemed to be its only purpose. Several meters away from the edge rose another wall, this one of wood. It had no windows or fingerholds; she couldn't climb higher. But neither were there any security devices around her. She was safe for the moment.

She closed her eyes and panted, wishing herself ten years younger, wishing she'd had all the latest physical upgrades.

"I'm on the roof just above the door," she said.

"Good. See anyone, or anything?"

She studied the yard before her. "No. Just the cameras."

"What about the tiles?"

"Slate," she said. "Very heavy."

"Try prying one out of position."

She pulled herself higher up, feeling for loose tiles. Finally she found one. Hooking her fingers under its edge, she heaved first one way, then another. Finally the tile came free. She lost her hold and nearly slid off the roof, but she managed to catch herself. Carefully she maneuvered to a more secure position. Then she tossed it into the bushes, where it landed with a dull *thump*.

Now the two tiles next to it were loose, and she worked on them quickly, eagerly. Bare wood lay underneath. Soon she'd exposed an area roughly half a meter square: large enough for her to get through, once the wood was gone.

She told Johnny as she drew a flamegun from her pack. It would ignite easily even in the rain, she knew. First she turned the flame down as low as it would go; then she closed her eyes, pointed the gun at the wood, and pulled the trigger.

Steam hissed; the burst of heat made her turn her head. The shot only lasted half a second, but it was enough to burn most of the way through the wood. It was little trouble to kick the charred remains away until she had an opening large enough to squeeze through. She dropped her pack into the darkness, gauged the distance, then lowered herself as well.

She was in an access area, she decided, as she crouched among dark rafters; she could feel wiring underfoot. She pulled up insulation and found ceiling tiles. It took only a moment to pull one up and lower herself to the floor.

Fortunately the foyer was empty. She turned off the door's security locks and monitors, then pulled it open.

Johnny was outside, dripping wet. He came in and shook the water from his clothes, then removed his mask and tucked it away. "Where's Jones's office?" he asked, as he rebolted the door.

"How would I know?"

"You've been here more than I have."

"I only saw the party rooms."

"Mm. Then we'll just have to look."

He dried himself as best he could on a curtain and she did the same, then led the way up the hall. At each door Johnny paused a moment, listened, studied the lock. Shelly shook her head; she didn't know what he was looking for.

Finally he stopped and said, "Ah! Finally."

"What?"

He pointed to a pinprick of red light next to the handpad. "This room has the most secure lock. Therefore there's something inside that Jones wants to protect, or something he doesn't want anyone else to see."

"Makes sense, I suppose."

Johnny grinned. Then he began working on the lock with a little silver tube from his pack. Rapidly spinning wires stuck out from one of its ends. At last tumblers clicked and the pinprick of red light turned green. With a flourish, Johnny pushed the door open and went in.

It was Jones's study, all right. A fireplace and bookshelves filled the wall to their left; to their right were several tall, ornate windows, with tapestries hanging between them. Half a dozen flowform chairs sat facing the huge realwood desk.

Shelly drew the curtains while Johnny sat at the desk and unfolded the computer terminal. After unlatching the front panel, he reached inside and pulled out a circuit board. From the pack he'd brought he took a number of small silver boxes that trailed wires. He fastened the wires to the circuit board, then turned on the terminal and sat back in the chair, watching, waiting.

A series of numbers and letters flashed across the screen. "He's using an old coding system," Johnny said after a moment's study. "It shouldn't take the program long to crack it."

As he said it, the screen went dark, then flashed on again with an option menu. Johnny leaned forward and keyed in several sequences of numbers faster than Shelly could follow. An instant later patterns of lines began flashing across the screen. They were blueprints, she realized a second later.

Johnny looked up. "The safe's over there," he said, pointing to the right. Rising, he strode over to the fireplace, made a quick examination of it, then depressed a brick.

Silently, a section of the wall pulled back, then slid aside to reveal a metal door with an old-fashioned tumbler.

"Shit," Johnny said, "the bastard used a mechanical lock!"

"So?"

"So how am I supposed to open it?"

"Let me."

"Don't burn it open," Johnny said. "That might destory the data on whatever's inside. Some chips can't stand heat."

"Yeah, sure," Shelly said. "Will plastics do?"

"Won't that raise an alarm?"

"Sure. But we can be out of here before anyone arrives."

Slowly he nodded. "Okay. But fast!"

Silently Shelly pulled a cube of plastic explosive from her pack, molded it into a circle, and pressed it against the safe. It stuck. Then she attached the detonator, set the time for fifteen seconds, and ran for cover.

Johnny joined her behind the desk. They covered their ears and ducked as low as they could.

With a loud *whump*, the plastics exploded. Papers scattered across the room; dust sifted from the ceiling. Fortunately, none of the windows broke and no audible alarms went off.

Johnny stood and hurried to the safe. The door hung from only one hinge; he pried it open. Inside were stacks of papers, thick bundles of newdollars, and several dozen memory bars.

He scooped up the bars and returned to the terminal. "Get the money," he said.

"What?" Shelly demanded. "Why?"

"It will confuse matters, make him wonder if the thieves were only after money. Especially when we leave the memory bars here."

Shelly made room in her pack and began stuffing in as much of the cash as she could. She noticed, with little surprise, that most of the bills were thousands and ten thousands.

"Found the codes!" Johnny announced. "Just a phone call to Nexus, then I'll dump them into the system."

"Hurry," Shelly said. "I can't imagine them missing the explosion, alarms or not."

"The room is probably soundproofed, considering what Jones has been up to. . . ."

Shelly nodded. "Could be."

He unplugged the vidphone, then jacked one of his silver boxes into the outgoing line. After keying in a sequence of numbers, he plugged the memory bars into various slots in his boxes. "Got to send Nexus the codes," he said. With a grand gesture, he pushed a small red button. The box whirred for half a second, then began beeping.

"Shit!" Johnny said, a startled look on his face.

"What's that?" Shelly said, tensing.

"That paranoid bastard put an alarm on his outgoing vid-phone line! Every SecurNet man still up'll be on our backs any second."

Shelly picked up her pack and began sorting through it. "I'll get you time to finish sending the codes."

"I'm done."

She looked at him. "Already?"

He removed the bars and tossed them to her. "Put them in the safe while I pack."

Shelly crossed to the safe and put the memory bars back where they'd found them. She forced the safe door back into position, then swung the fireplace back in front; it sealed without leaving a trace of the damage.

Johnny had stuffed everything back into his pack by then. "Move it!" he said, starting for the door.

Shelly reached into her pack for her pistol. Better be ready to fight, she thought, now that the alarm was given.

An instant later the door crashed open. Two men in Se-curNet uniforms stood there, rifles drawn.

All elected government officials are, by nature, cowards. They must maintain a pleasant, competent, thoroughly noncommittal facade at all times... strong positions on controversial issues might well put their position at risk. Remember, however, that despite their appearance, these are men of subtlety and deceit; do not turn your back on them or their servants will take you down.

—John Zedowski
Long Summer Days

—17—

RATHER than draw her pistol, Shelly looped her finger through one of the gas grenades' pullrings as she turned.

"I have a frag grenade with a three-second delay," she said, drawing it out so they could see. Other than the cloud symbol—which she covered with her thumb—there was no way for them to know she wasn't telling the truth. "It'll make a mess out of everyone in this room. If you shoot, I'll still end up pulling the pin. You'll be dogmeat, too."

"Standoff?" the first SecurNet guard said. Then he laughed. "Reinforcements are on the way. This room gets cleared out whether we're dead or not."

"Then we'd better—" Shelly said, pulling out the grenade's pin, "all die now."

The two SecurNet guards yelped and dove for cover behind two of the flowform chairs facing the desk. Johnny just gaped at her.

Shelly tossed the grenade toward the guards' side of the room and launched herself at Johnny. The two of them went down, Shelly on top, as one of the SecurNet men opened fire. Plastic fléchettes raked across the room. Glass shattered; metal pinged; wood splintered. Shelly felt something like a baseball bat pound across her left side but ignored it and scrambled behind the desk, pulling Johnny with her.

The grenade went off with a loud *pop*, then a hissing sound. There were curses from the two SecurNet men.

"Quickly," Shelly said, struggling with her backpack. Her left arm felt alternately hot and cold; it was slick with blood, numb to near uselessness. She'd been hit, she realized suddenly. "Get out the breathers," she said. She gulped in one last lungful of air, then held it.

Johnny pulled himself to his knees and rummaged through the various weapons in her pack until he pulled out two plastic circlets. He pulled one over his own head and took the bit in his mouth, then pulled the other one over Shelly's head, too. She tongued the mouthpiece into comfortable position, then allowed herself to breathe again, rasping through the filters.

The air around them had taken on a milky, opalescent quality. The SecurNet guards would be out cold from the gas by now, Shelly knew. How long would it take for their reinforcements to arrive?

"Roll over," Johnny said, voice muffled.

Shelly complied. Now that she looked, she could see the bright blue endtabs of seven fléchettes protruding from her left arm, chest, hip, and thigh—she'd caught part of a round as she dove at Johnny. Worse, that whole side of her body felt weak and heavy: the fléchettes had been drug-tipped. She'd never be able to walk out of here now.

Johnny shook his head. "That's bad, Shel."

"Ditch me. You've got the codes, so don't risk getting caught—just get out of here!"

"Jones'll kill you."

"Do it."

He rose, glanced at the door, then back down at her. "The guards are unconscious. We've got time—"

"Run, you stupid shit! You heard them say it—they've called for help. Run!"

He hesitated, looking back at her and then at the door, and she could see the pain in his face.

"Run!" she screamed at him.

He did it. He scooped up the backpacks and fled, leaving her there alone. Shelly listened until she couldn't hear his pounding footsteps anymore, then began crying softly, from the pain, from the hurt inside. It made sense for him to go, she told herself over and over. Rationally he had to escape. It would be stupid for him to try to rescue her—she was just muscle, after all, easily replaced. He, on the other hand, was important, vital; the revolution needed him. But somehow she longed for him to have stayed, to have argued longer, to have *tried* in some way.

Slowly, with her one working arm and one working leg, she dragged herself around the corner of the desk. With every movement her wounds howled their pain, the fléchettes digging even more deeply into her flesh. Her senses seemed to expand until she saw and heard everything with unnatural clarity. At last she'd pulled herself into a position from which she could see the doorway.

The two SecurNet guards lay out in the open, sprawled across the carpet. One was snoring softly. She watched his chest move as he breathed, up and down, up and down.

As the minutes ticked away, her despair lifted a bit. Johnny'd always said you weren't out of a fight until you were dead. Well, she certainly wasn't dead yet. Almost, but not quite; that meant she still had a chance.

She heard footsteps in the hallway and for an instant her heart leaped—Johnny'd come back for her! But then she heard more, the tramp of boots on oak flooring, low voices calling deployment orders, and she knew the truth: it had to be more SecurNet guards coming to reinforce the two she'd gassed.

Play dead, she thought. *I'll let them in, then kill them all.* A frag grenade would smear the lot. When she reached for her backpack and didn't find it, she remembered Johnny taking it. She cursed. That left her completely unarmed.

She lay back and waited. They wouldn't question her if they thought she were unconscious: that was the best plan. They'd probably just dump her into a holding cell in a SecurNet prison, where torturers would worm the truth out of her bit by bit. She'd fight it, of course, but in the end she knew she'd spill, tell them everything she knew about Johnny and Karl and Nexus and Tech House. Johnny should've killed her before he left, she realized. That would have solved everything. Why hadn't she thought of it? Now she just hoped to buy enough time for the techs to pull off the transfer.

Eyes slitted, she watched the first two guards slip through the door, moving low, rifles ready. They were decked out in complete body armor, with goggles and gas masks. After making a quick circuit of the room, tearing down curtains and tapestries, looking behind all the furniture, they checked their fallen comrades. Then they came and glanced over Shelly's wounds, but didn't touch her. Shelly knew what they were thinking, though: she was unarmed, badly wounded, and therefore of no immediate threat.

One of them shut down the security locks and rolled open the windows. A breeze stirred the air; the sleepgas began to dissipate.

"Clear," one of them said to the microphone at his collar.

Two more SecurNet guards entered, rifles held ready, and one of these was an officer by the gold braid at this shoulder. The officer came over to Shelly, bent down, felt her pulse. After a moment, he skinned back one of her eyelids.

Shelly let her thoughts drift. She didn't move a muscle, didn't let her breathing quicken.

"Give me the pliers from your pack," he said to one of the others. "She'll talk soon enough."

Shelly felt a tremor of fear run like a live wire down her spine. Heart pounding in her throat, guts all twisting into knots, she suddenly realized what he meant to do. He was going to pull out the fléchettes one by one. It was crude, very crude. And it would be a hell for her.

"What's going on here?" a strong, familiar voice said from the doorway.

Shelly moved her eyes a fraction to take in the door. It was Johnny, she saw, come back after stashing their packs. He wasn't armed, and somehow he'd changed clothes, was wearing a black SecurNet uniform. He hadn't ditched her after all! She felt both angry and thankful at once and didn't know which was more important.

"Sir! I hadn't realized you were here." The officer stood and saluted smartly. "We have a prisoner, sir. She broke in and managed to gas two of our boys, but not before they took her out."

"Good work," Johnny said. He sneered at Shelly, every

inch the SecurNet commander he was. "Have you called an ambulance yet?"

"No, sir. I was about to question her, then make my report to HQ."

"Good, good. Carry on."

"Yes, sir." The officer took the pliers offered by one of the other SecurNet guards, then looked down and nudged Shelly with the toe of his boot. "Got anything to say before I start my work?"

But Shelly was more interested in what Johnny was doing. He'd reached to the side of the door and pulled out her automatic rifle. In an instant he'd snapped it up, finger squeezing the trigger. He fanned the room with a ten-second burst of knifebullets.

The four SecurNet men seemed to leap across the room, smashing into the far wall, chests shredding like paper. They didn't have time to scream, let alone shoot back. Their mouths gaped; blood poured from their wounds. Slowly they collapsed to the floor, so much fresh meat. The wall behind them was smeared a brilliant crimson.

Johnny shouldered the rifle and jogged over to Shelly. "I couldn't leave you," he said simply.

"You— I . . . I mean, thank you," Shelly said.

He lifted her up and managed to half-drag her, awkwardly, out to the hallway. Pain jabbed at Shelly with every movement, but she gritted her teeth and managed to keep silent. Once she looked back and noticed the trail of blood she was leaving. Couldn't be helped now, she thought. The feet already had a sample, anyway: anyone who checked would just come up with a match for a known Disruptionist.

Johnny said, "There's a small aircar parked on the roof, and the keys are inside . . . I checked. We'll get out that way."

The hall seemed to be spinning around and around like a gyroscope. Johnny lifting her, his arms strong and sure. And, pulled tight against his chest, Shelly heard his heart beating, loud and steady, and knew he couldn't fail.

She closed her eyes and felt darkness unfolding around her.

There is no such thing as a perfect government. The closest to perfection Man has yet come is a benign dictatorship. Government by committee has always led to corruption, and always will.

—John Zedowski
The Upstairs Room

—18—

WHEN Shelly next opened her eyes, the world blurred and rippled. Bright lights and the smell of antiseptic surrounded her, and among the lights moved dark phantom shapes. Muted voices, as though coming from a great distance, seemed to be discussing her condition. Yes, it was definitely men she heard talking . . . was Johnny among them?

Her thoughts drifted for a time. Finally someone lifted her; something cold touched the nape of her neck, making her shiver convulsively. Then a burst of warmth flooded through her body, spreading to her arms and legs, to her fingers and toes. Her spinal cord had been reconnected, she realized then. She sat up and her vision cleared.

She was in an operating theater, she noted, with various steel instruments to her left and right. A shadow fell over her. Looking up, she saw a dogman's whiskered face peering down at her. His tongue lolled out; he panted.

"Uh, hello," Shelly said.

"Woof?"

There was something familiar about him. "I remember you," Shelly said slowly. "You're Paul. Yeah. You work for Esteban Grammatica." She tried to sit up; Paul used his paws to help her.

"Done now," he said. "The master's best work."

"Thanks." She just sat there for a minute, breathing deeply. The dogman bounded to the other side of the room and began folding surgical tools into the wall with practiced efficiency.

They'd done a quick rebuild on her body, Shelly thought, repairing the fléchette wounds and flushing the paralysis drug from her muscle tissue. That she was naked seemed almost an afterthought.

She flexed arms and legs, found them tinglingly alive. After running her fingers over the skin where the fléchettes had hit, she decided that Grammatica had done a superb job once more. Other than a few tender spots, she couldn't find a trace of her wounds. The skin grafts matched so perfectly she couldn't even tell where they began, half the time.

"Ah, Shelly Tracer!" Esteban Grammatica swept in through the door, his voice oily smooth as ever. "I am so happy to see you up and awake, yes!"

"Thanks," Shelly said. "I appreciate all you did."

He shrugged a little, feigning modesty. "Your body is my canvas, and it is always a pleasure to create a work of beauty. Now, perhaps just a small final touch . . . fish scales, perhaps? To accent the lines of your skin? Yes?" His eyes shifted to take in her breasts, the shape of her legs. "Yes," he whispered, hands drifting down, "definitely fish scales, *here* and *here*, and perhaps *here*?"

Shelly pushed him away. "Not my style, and your hands are cold." She turned, noticed a white robe on a hook by the door. Putting it on and knotting the belt, she glanced the room over once more. "I suppose you no longer have my clothes?"

"So many holes in them, yes! I judged them far beyond repair." Laughing, he took her arm, fingers circling tightly around her wrist. His reptilian touch made her skin crawl, but Shelly didn't dare risk offending him by drawing away; no telling when she'd need his services again. "Come," he said. "Zed is outside, waiting for you. He is so impatient, yes!"

She accompanied him to the showroom, with its constantly bubbling tanks of animal parts. As he'd said, scales seemed the rule of the day. She noticed flashprints of fishmen and snakemen decorating the walls, and overhead in shimmering primal colors swam holosnakes and holofish.

Johnny nodded as he looked Shelly over. "It seems you did a passable job this time, Grammatica."

"Passable?" the snakeman snapped. "*Passable?* She is a work of art! My finest grafting, my greatest musclemeshing, my most intricate nerve work! *Passable!*"

"Johnny wouldn't use you if you weren't the best," Shelly told him. "He knows it."

"Bill Tech House, as usual," Johnny said, tossing Shelly a small bundle. It was a black daysuit, she saw. "Get dressed," he told her. "We have things to do."

Ten minutes later they were safely underground in Tech House, in the room with walls filled with vidscreens. Anne Bonny and Rad Lad were lying on the couches at the center of the room while Liberator and

Mask moved along the railed walk, keying numbers into the pads they carried.

Johnny almost leaped down the stairs to the computer terminal next to the couches. He sat before it, then typed a brief message.

A moment later Rad Lad disconnected himself from the system and sat up. His eyes glowed brilliantly white; quickly he put on dark glasses. "Yours, Johnny," he said, grinning. "The grunt work is done. What is left remains for you now." Stretching, he stood and moved aside, brushing the wrinkles from his white robes.

Johnny lay down and closed his eyes. Shelly watched as little wires wormed their way up from the couch's fabric and into his hair, entering his skull in a dozen places. It made her faintly uneasy, but there was nothing to be done about it; besides, if all went well, it would be over in an afternoon. Then she wouldn't have to think about Johnny's brain being wired into machines.

Shelly sat next to Rad Lad and stared at the vidscreen opposite her. It blacked out, then numbers began flashing past almost too quickly for her to follow. She recognized a few address codes; Johnny was finding the proper bank.

Then the screen flickered, jumping with sparks and static, and a blinking cursor appeared against a backdrop of snaking green lines. Slowly numbers appeared: the first of the access codes they'd stolen.

The screen blinked twice, then the cursor disappeared. The lines flowed past in a torrent, then abruptly took shape in what appeared to be a surrealist's nightmare: red spheres floating against a backdrop of wavy green. Each sphere had its own code number, she noted. Point of view was changing ever so slightly, coasting them forward through the green like a man passing through a series of curtains.

Now, Shelly saw, there were dark patches on the screen, places where the pattern was shaded or missing altogether. It was toward one of these patches that Johnny seemed to be heading.

Nervous, Shelly looked at Rad Lad. She'd heard about the dangers of breaking into banking systems and knew there would be safeguards to keep thieves such as Johnny from transferring funds. But the dark patches didn't seem to bother Rad Lad, at least not yet, so she relaxed. It wouldn't do to disturb Johnny's concentration by shouting a warning, she thought, not when a microsecond could be the difference between success and failure. Not when there might not be anything to worry about.

The screen froze for an instant; another blinking cursor appeared. Johnny input another of the access codes. Suddenly the dark patch disappeared, becoming another of the red spheres. It had been hidden, Shelly realized, inaccessible to them—the dark patches were shields of some kind.

New lines rippled across the sphere's surface; it grew larger, more distinct, until its image filled the vidscreen. It resembled a globe of a planet more than anything else, she thought, with thousands of lines of latitude and longitude. Wine-colored splotches that could have been continents marred its surface; pinpricks of brighter red could easily have marked volcanoes, or missile sites, or any of a thousand landmarks.

Johnny zoomed in on one pinprick. It became another glowing green curtain of lines, dotted with more red spheres. Numbers streamed across the bottom third of the viewscreen. Again Johnny entered more access codes.

Rad Lad suddenly jerked to his feet. An instant later Shelly saw what had alerted him: a dark slug-shape of blue lines, denser than the green curtain, was inching its way across the face of the sphere. It made her uneasy, like watching a spider stalking across its web.

"What's that?" she demanded, not taking her eyes from it.

"A trap of some kind. Johnny sees it, though."

"How can you tell?"

"He is backing off."

Sure enough, the red sphere diminished in size until it filled less than half the vidscreen. The blue slug continued its slow crawl, watching, waiting.

Words appeared across the vidscreen—

TAKE ANNE BONNY OUT OF NEXUS; PATCH HER IN HERE. SHE CAN TRY TO GO IN, ATTRACT ITS ATTENTION. WHEN IT JUMPS HER, I WILL SLIP PAST.

Rad Lad sat back down and typed an answer at the terminal, then addressed Anne Bonny through the system. A moment later, Anne gave a little moan and stirred; then she settled back and a blank expression came over her face.

"She is now following Johnny's trail," Rad Lad said. "Her projection should appear in a second."

Shelly nodded. As she did, a shapeless white glow came into view in the vidscreen's lower right-hand corner. It inched toward the slug on the red sphere.

"Easy there," Rad Lad whispered.

Suddenly the slug leaped toward Anne Bonny. Johnny didn't hesitate; he zipped in close to the red sphere. Again the red lines appeared, the red continents, the red sparks. One of the sparks grew to fill the screen. Lines rippled; viewpoint shifted. Then they seemed to be looking down on a table covered with moving balls of light. This time, though, the balls were all racing toward one another, faster and faster; and when they collided they merged with a surge of light. When the light faded, all the balls vanished; the table was empty.

"First account closed," Rad Lad whispered, studying the terminal in front of him. "Thirteen trillion dollars deposited into our account."

Gasping, Anne Bonny suddenly sat up. Sweat streamed down her face; her mouth opened and closed soundlessly.

Shelly raced forward to help her, but Anne raised her hand. "No," she said. "It's always disconcertin' when y're thrust from a system. I'll be right soon 'nuf." She lay back and jacked into the system once more.

More slowly, Shelly rejoined Rad Lad.

"She has gone back to service Nexus accounts," Rad Lad said. "Do not worry; she is too good to get brainwiped in a trap."

"Yeah, I should've known," Shelly said. Sitting, she turned her attention to the vidscreen again.

Johnny had selected a second red spark and was busy rounding up the red spheres . . . subaccounts. It looked like it was going to be a long night, Shelly thought. She didn't dare take her eyes off the vidscreen for more than a moment. There was no telling when Johnny or Rad Lad or any of the others might need her.

Three hours later, the congressional accounts wiped clear of stolen money, Johnny disconnected.

It was the law of averages, Shelly decided: so much had gone wrong already—from the Disruption to the alarm in Jones's house to the shootout with the SecurNet guards— that something *had* to work for them. Luckily it was this last, most important mission.

In those three hours Johnny had transferred 714 trillion newdollars to Nexus's accounts. Rad Lad had kept a running total.

Johnny grinned widely. He was bleary-eyed, his movements sluggish, but there was pride and triumph in his voice as he said, "We did it!"

"Yeah!" Shelly said. "Faster than I thought, and smooth."

"Tomorrow's the day, then," Johnny said. "I'm scheduled to make a routine report on SecurNet. But instead I'll reveal the theft."

"You're sure it'll work?" Shelly said.

"Of course." He smiled, confident, serene. "When have I ever been wrong?"

Rising, he bade her good night and went to the lift. Anne Bonny remained in the system. Nexus still had a business to run, Shelly had to keep reminding herself. But soon they wouldn't have to worry about it anymore.

Shelly spent a restless night alone in her room. Despite so much going on, despite having done so much that day, she found her thoughts racing along faster than ever. Johnny and Karl, Rad Lad and the Disruption—they were all moving too quickly for her. For a moment she let herself wish for the simpler days of her childhood, when politics had been nothing more than a vague subject to be studied through history vids in school. Now that things had come to a climax, now that Congress might actually fall to Johnny's plan, everything seemed more complicated than ever before.

And what of her? Where would she fit into the new system? What place would there be for a violent revolutionary whose violent revolution had succeeded? It was a matter of change, she told herself. Once, long ago, she'd thought that destroying Congress's powerbase would let her return to normal society. Later she'd thought that the Disruption could well be a lifetime work. Now that the end had moved into sight, she couldn't help but wonder whether she'd belong in the new American society at all.

What had the Russians done after their revolution? Hadn't they killed off most of the hard-core revolutionaries?

She shook her head. There were a few obvious parallels, but most comparisons between her America and old Russia simply wouldn't work. The world had changed too much, and, anyway, American society had never been like the Russians'.

On the bright side, she didn't think Johnny ruthless enough to kill her. Hadn't he rescued her twice when he shouldn't have? If he'd really wanted to get rid of her, he could've done it easily when he betrayed the Disruption.

Finally, after hours of confused wondering, she dozed off.

When she woke, it was eleven o'clock in the morning. Rising, she dialed a skimpy meal from the autochef, dressed while it was cooking, then ate and hurried down to the common room to join the others.

As she entered, she sensed the tension in the room immediately. Johnny's face was on the wall vidphone; he was calling from Karl's aircar.

"Good morning, Shel," he said, smiling.

"Yeah, thanks," she said. "Where are you?"

"The Congressional Complex. I have to give my report this morning, remember?"

"I didn't think it would be this early."

"It is." He glanced at his watch. "In fact, I've got to run if I'm to make it in time. Wish me luck."

"You've never needed luck before."

He grinned. "Then wish me skill."

"I wish you success."

"Even better." He looked at Rad Lad. "Is everything ready for you to patch in when necessary?"

"Hmm? Of course. We have gone over the schedule too often not to be prepared."

"Just checking. Everything must go as planned if it's to work. Until this afternoon, then." He severed the connection.

Rad Lad switched to the NewsNets and flicked through them until he came to one covering the Congressional Assembly. Coverage was general, little more than direct broadcasts of speeches, with a commentator to fill the gaps.

Shelly settled back and used the controls in the chair's arm to adjust its padding. Rad Lad and Anne Bonny were sitting to her right, Lord Hathgar and Liberator to her left. She watched the vidscreen's reflection on their glasses for a moment, wondering what they thought of Johnny's fight, wondering what he'd done to win their respect and loyalty, how he'd ever gotten mixed up with techs in the first place. Finally she sighed and turned her full attention to the vid.

The woman speaking at the podium finished to polite applause, then stepped down. The camera panned as Johnny Zed entered; it followed him up the aisle.

"This is it," Rad Lad said. He upped the volume.

Johnny took his position at the podium. Setting his sheath of papers down, he spread them out before him and took the first. Clearing his throat, he began to read:

"It has come to my attention as head of SecurNet that vast amounts of money have been removed from congressional accounts over the last few years—slightly more than seven-hundred-*trillion* dollars in all. This stolen money has been used to buy congressmen huge estates, month-long trips to European pleasure palaces, and other personal luxuries.

"This theft is an act of betrayal against the American people. It can only be viewed as treason. I have before me a list of the perpetrators of this most heinous crime. Foremost among the thieves is the Speaker of the—"

He cut off amid popping sounds, and the vidcamera swung crazily to take in all of Congress. Men and women were on their feet, shouting. Several waved handguns even though weapons were illegal in congressional assemblies. Shelly found herself on her feet, too, a sick fear jumping through her guts like an electric current.

"No," she whispered. "No, no, no."

The camera finally swung back to the podium. Johnny was lying on his side. The vid zoomed in on his face, and Shelly could see his lips moving ever so faintly, could read the surprise in his eyes. *Congressmen never get their own hands dirty.* He'd said it a thousand times. But he'd been wrong. It had only taken one who was different, one who was daring. It had only taken one to shoot him down and prove him wrong.

A trickle of blood ran from the corner of Johnny's mouth. SecurNet guards were bending over him now, shielding his body with theirs, trying to help. They blocked the vid's view so Shelly couldn't see. Her fingernails bit into her palms; she gnawed on her lip in frustration. Medics in white were rushing up to the podium now, bags of instruments in their hands.

Finally the people shifted and she could see Johnny coughing up blood and spittle. There was blood all over his chest and face now, pooling across the floor. He half-moaned, half-wheezed as they lifted him onto a stretcher. It was a pathetic hurt-dog sound, and it tore at her. Then a glazed look came over Johnny's face and he lay still, eyes open, staring endlessly.

"He's dead," she heard one of the medics say. There was bewilderment in his tone. Then people were blocking the camera again and Shelly couldn't see Johnny Zed anymore.

Not that it mattered. Not that anything mattered. Johnny was *dead*. She didn't want to believe it, couldn't believe it. She sank back, tears coming to her eyes. There was an awful silence in the room.

"It's over," Rad Lad said finally. "Kill the feed."

"No," Shelly said. She swung around. "Patch it in." Her voice was wild, straining. "Do it *now!*"

Lord Hathgar looked from her to Rad Lad and back again, as if he didn't know who to obey. Finally he fitted a wire into the jack in the side of his head, then leaned back in his seat. The scene of Congress flashed off, replaced by a test pattern, then text began to scroll as a voice read:

THE DAY HAS COME TO AWAKEN TO THE CRIMES OF CONGRESS. OVER SEVEN HUNDRED TRILLION DOLLARS OF TAX MONEY HAS BEEN SECRETLY STOLEN BY A GROUP OF EIGHTY-FIVE LEADING SENATORS AND REPRESENTATIVES. THIS MONEY LAY IN CAREFULLY GUARDED SWISS ACCOUNTS UNTIL EARLY THIS MORNING, WHEN IT WAS STOLEN BACK BY MEMBERS OF SECURNET. THIS MONEY IS NOW BEING HELD IN ESCROW FOR THE PEOPLE OF THE UNITED STATES OF AMERICA AND WILL BE TURNED OVER TO A DULY ELECTED PRESIDENT FOR USE IN REBUILDING THE EXECUTIVE BRANCH OF THE GOVERNMENT. NOW IS THE TIME TO MAKE YOUR PRESENCE FELT. NOW IS THE TIME TO ELIMINATE THE THIEVES AND CRIMINALS KNOWN AS CONGRESS. MAKE YOUR VOICE HEARD. HERE IS A LIST OF THE CONGRESSMEN KNOWN TO BE INVOLVED IN THE THEFTS—

and the names began to appear. After they had all run past, the message began to repeat itself.

"I can't believe he's dead," Shelly said. There was a

yawning emptiness within her, as though a hole to infinity had suddenly opened in her chest. Her head ached; she leaned forward and cradled it in her hands.

"It does seem a bit unreal," Rad Lad said. "But life goes on. Now we have other things to worry about, other things to do. People will be tracing Johnny's movements. Doubtless that will bring them here to Tech House."

Shelly stared at him, scarcely able to believe what she'd heard. "Don't you *care* what happened to him?" she demanded.

"Of course. But we must think of ourselves first. That means we must cut from Tech House. Shelter can be gotten from other houses easily enough for us. But you . . ."

"So that's it, is it?" Shelly said.

"Yes." Rad Lad rose, started for the door.

"Congress has caught our broadcast," Anne Bonny said from across the room. Her voice was cool, uninvolved. "They've ordered the NewsNets censored."

Rad Lad turned, looked at her. "And?"

"I've blocked their attempts." She sneered. "Clumsy."

Liberator said, "They have now called a closed congressional meeting."

"What about Karl?" Shelly asked.

"He is there. Yes. He will let us know what happens."

Shelly leaned back. Her legs felt weak; she took a shuddering breath and forced herself to stand. Academically she knew what had happened: Johnny had guessed wrong about Congress, guessed wrong about the senators and representatives dirtying their own hands. Now Rad Lad wanted to cut his losses, ditch Tech House, run. Shelly couldn't blame him: it was practical from anyone's point of view. But her emotions still churned; she wasn't ready to accept defeat.

Congressmen never dirty their own hands. That's what SecurNet was for. How could they have killed him?

She cursed them all.

"Come," Rad Lad said, and the others stood and began shutting down the equipment. "We can set up elsewhere soon enough."

"No," Shelly said. She whipped around to look at him. Her anger was hot now, and wild, barely in check. "We're going to fight. Congress can still be beaten."

"Not," Rad Lad said, "by us. Think of the money we now have. *Seven hundred and fourteen trillion dollars*. Think of the power it will buy. It is time to forget Congress and move on to more important things. Let the matter die with Johnny."

Shelly stood, fists on the table, and leaned forward until her face was scant centimeters from his. *"Never."*

CONGRESS: FOLLOWING THIS MORNING'S REVELATION
THAT SEVEN HUNDRED TRILLION DOLLARS HAS BEEN
STOLEN FROM CONGRESSIONAL ACCOUNTS BY A CON-
SORTIUM OF 85 CONGRESSMEN, CONGRESS HAS VOTED
TO STEP DOWN AS THE GOVERNING BODY OF THE
UNITED STATES OF AMERICA. A PRESIDENT AND VICE
PRESIDENT WILL BE APPOINTED TO HEAD THE NEW
UNITED STATES GOVERNMENT UNTIL ELECTIONS CAN
BE HELD. AS OF THIS TIME TOMORROW, CONGRESS WILL
RESUME ITS FORMER POSITION AS A PURELY LEGISLA-
TIVE BODY.

   FOR RELATED STORIES, SEE: 1) JOHN ZEDOWSKI
(10952561-A); 2) ASSASSINATION IN CONGRESS (10952782-
A; 3) CONGRESSIONAL FUNDS MISSING (10952814-A)

−30−

—19—

RAD Lad laughed at her. "You are as much of a
dreamer as Johnny ever was. So be it. Stay and
fight; none here will stop you."

He turned to go. Shelly was around the desk and racing
for him a heartbeat later. It was a gut-level reaction, faster
than thought. She had no plan—just raw anger.

She tackled his legs. Dark glasses flying, he sprawled
across the carpet. Cursing, Shelly flipped him over, pinned
his arms with her knees. One hand closed around his
throat. The other drew back in a fist.

"No!" Rad Lad begged, trying to twist away. "Do not

181

strike me—too many delicate upgrades inside my head—
you might damage them—"

Shelly tightened her grip until he gasped for breath.
Then she leaned forward and peered into the mirrors of his
eyes. Her reflection was bloated, changed. Her voice iced
as she said, "I'm going to the Congressional Complex."

"Yes—any—thing—you—want—"

"You're going to give me the weapons I need."

"No—"

She choked off his protest. Finally he nodded and she
relaxed her grip again. Releasing him, she stood. He began
wheezing, trying to draw in great gulps of air.

"Get up," she said. She looked at the others; none of
them had moved an inch during the fight. She sneered; no
loyalty. Techs were worse than streeters when it came to
that.

Rad Lad rolled over and started puking on the floor.
When he was done he just lay there, moaning softly.

Shelly grabbed him by his shirt, pulled him to his knees.
"Get *up!*"

"You are wrong," he whispered, drooling a bit. "You
cannot fight Congress. SecurNet will cut you down."

"Congress upped the stakes," she said. "Now it's my
turn. That's the way you fight a war if you want to win—
they pull a gun, we pull a missile. Simple."

His eyes widened. "You can't—"

"I *will*."

She could see the portable missile launcher in Tech
House's arsenal. She could see that and all the other explosives stored there. Now, with Congress in a closed meeting, it would only take one direct hit to wipe them all out
of existence. . . .

She smiled sweetly. "The plan will go on as Johnny
wanted," she said to the others. "Continue monitoring
Congress. Don't let them trace Johnny back here."

"Easy 'nuf," Anne Bonny said. She sat back down and jacked into the system.

To Liberator, Shelly said, "Have Karl's aircar come by to pick me up. There must be a loading bay for the arsenal. Bring it in there."

Liberator looked at Rad Lad, who nodded ever so slightly. "Very well," he said.

Shelly took Rad Lad's arm and forcibly got him moving. In the hallway, with the door closed, Shelly found herself starting to crash from her adrenaline high. *Johnny's dead.* She drew a shuddering breath and tightened her grip on Rad Lad's arm until he squealed in protest.

She forced a smile. "I know what you're thinking," she said, even though she hadn't the faintest idea. "Don't try it. You'll only end up dead."

He glowered at her. Then the lift arrived and Shelly pulled him in, then hit the button for the arsenal.

On the way down, she released him. She couldn't go around holding his hand the rest of her life, she thought. She had better things to do, more important things to do.

"Try anything and I'll kill you," she said.

"You will regret these actions."

"Yeah. I've regretted a lot of things lately."

He stared at the wall, motionless, utterly silent. He could've been a statue in his white robe. Shelly sighed. When the doors opened, she pushed him out into the hallway, heading for the arsenal. Inside, from the doorway, she marveled once more at all the weapons he'd managed to gather. But it was the missiles that interested her most right now.

She started toward the missile launchers, Rad Lad in front of her, both of them weaving their way among the crates. Shelly noticed how he didn't look at any of the weapons they were passing. His actions were too deliberate, she thought; he had something planned.

When Shelly passed a rack of rifles, she silently scooped one up, made sure the clip was full, thumbed off the safety. She was quiet as a ghost, fast as only a pro can be.

Ten steps farther, Rad Lad seized a pistol and whirled. But she was ready, had expected it. He stared at the rifle Shelly had pointed at his belly.

"Drop it," Shelly said.

He did so, very slowly. Then he raised his hands and waited in silence.

"Johnny trusted you," she said.

"Not without reason. He was the best. I learned from him most eagerly."

"There's more to life than that."

"You live only to learn, then to be the best yourself. That is a tech's life."

"You got screwed along the way."

"So it goes."

"I'm sorry," Shelly said. "I wish I could trust you."

He started to speak. She pulled the trigger, watched the bullets rip him apart. Blood sprayed like a fountain from his mouth. A second later Shelly released the trigger. Rad Lad just stood there. Slowly he sank to his knees, a glazed look on his face. When he fell forward, on his face, Shelly turned and continued over to the portable missile launchers.

They fired one-hundred-kilo missiles with impact heads and plastics cores—missiles designed for taking out large buildings with one hit. It would take several to destroy the congressional complex, Shelly thought—best to use six. That way there wouldn't be the slightest chance of any survivors.

With a grating roar, the back end of the room split in half and slid to the sides, revealing an immense freight elevator. Karl's aircar was parked there, the side hatch already open. Liberator and Karl's chauffeur, Lang, were standing beside it.

They both stared past her, at Rad Lad's body, saying nothing.

Shelly said, unnecessarily, "Rad Lad's dead."

Liberator said, "He was selfish. And a fool. One cannot live long with such a combination."

"And you're different?"

He inclined his head slightly. "We discussed the matter after you left with Rad Lad. Johnny wanted his revolution. We will give it to him, Anne and Mask and I . . . he deserves that much loyalty from us, considering all he did to support Tech House."

"You're not just saying that?"

"No."

Shelly believed him. The remaining techs could easily have bolted as soon as she'd left the common room with Rad Lad. All they had to do was call Lang to be picked up. In staying and volunteering to help, they had to be thinking of Johnny; they certainly didn't owe her any loyalty.

She said, "What about the others?"

"They will help, too."

She smiled. It was just as she'd thought. "Terrific. Help me with the missiles—we'll need to bundle them together in threes, then load them into the aircar on dollies. And I want to take incendiary bombs—and smokers—"

They bent to the task. It didn't take long to unload the missiles from their racks, rope them together, set them on wheeled carts, and maneuver them into place inside the aircar.

Liberator was sweating when they finished, panting for breath, his pale face flushed a bright red. Shelly realized he wasn't used to this kind of exertion. But then she'd always thought of techs as soft . . . Johnny had been the exception.

But then, Johnny had been an exception to almost everything.

After the incendiaries and smokers were aboard, Shelly climbed in with them. They took up much of the aircar's floor, and she moved carefully among them.

"Are you sure this is what you want?" Liberator said. "If SecurNet suspects—"

Lang laughed. "How would they, unless someone told them? I'm flying a senator's 'car, remember, and I have all the passcodes to get into congressional airspace. It's only right that I show up to pick up the senator."

Shelly said, "I'm sure you can think of some way to further inconvenience SecurNet—can't you blank out their computer system while we're flying over?"

Liberator shook his head. "Too tricky; that would take weeks of planning, weeks of scouting through their computer system. And, if we did it, their first reaction might be to attack—to shoot down anything that might be a possible threat. Including you."

"Yeah, I guess. Well, try to think of something, even if it's only a minor distraction."

"We will try," he said doubtfully. "But don't count on any distractions."

Shelly turned to Lang. "Let's go."

The ride was as draining as any Shelly had ever taken before a Disruptionist hit. She kept worrying about whether SecurNet would pass them (though she knew, deep inside, that they would), whether the techs would keep their word, whether the missiles would work. And, through it all, she kept seeing Johnny lying before Congress, dying. Why did it have to hurt so much? It was just like Harran dying all over again, only worse. Why had she cared about Johnny? He'd used her, he'd made her a means to his ends. But it had been more than that, too. Once more she could feel his arms about her as he lifted her, carried her from Jones's house. He must've loved her, too, to save her. Just as she'd loved him.

When she looked at the six missiles, at the incendiary bombs, at the smokers and other explosives bundled together to be dropped on the congressional complex, she prayed it would be enough.

"How long will it be before we reach the complex?" she asked Lang over the intercom.

"An hour," he said. "Anne Bonny advises you to check the NewsNets. There is rioting at a number of banks."

"Thanks." She sat back and flipped on the vid. Perhaps it would keep her mind occupied until they got there.

Sure enough, the first NewsNet she came to had live coverage. Aircar vidcrews hovered over a street where literally hundreds of men and women pushed and shoved their way toward an already packed bank. Fights had broken out in the center. She saw flashes of light as handguns were fired.

Then there were SecurNet guards parachuting down, and feet squads rolling up in ground vehicles. Gas grenades went off; people at the fringes of the crowd began to bolt for safety that wasn't there. SecurNet guards were all too busy using steel clubs and knives to restore order.

Good, Shelly thought grimly, leaning back. *This'll keep SecurNet occupied, at least*. She could imagine the SecurNet guards at the congressional complex all clustered around vids, watching the rioting, cheering as one of their comrades clubbed down another streeter.

Finally the intercom clicked, sounding like a pistol being cocked. "Almost there," Lang told her. Then she could hear him giving the passcodes to the SecurNet forces on the ground.

Shelly stood, swaying slightly. The aircar's hull vibrated underfoot. She took a rope from the pile of equipment she'd brought and tied one end to the metal railing beside the table, then tied the other end around her waist; when she opened the hatch to dump the missiles, she didn't want to take a chance on getting blown out herself.

She looked out one of the windows. The congressional complex was still half a kilometer away; they were circling in a holding pattern. Clearance must have been given for them, for abruptly they banked and headed for the complex at a leisurely pace, like any other aircar coming to pick up a congressman.

At two hundred meters away, Shelly pulled up on the hatch's handle. At once a red light blinked overhead and a recorded voice said, "This vehicle is still in flight. It is dangerous to open the hatch. This vehicle is still—"

She forced the handle the rest of the way, heard a glass securlock rod break. Then the hatch swung open and air whipped over her.

She swung uneasily from the handle for a moment, then grabbed the rope around her waist with one hand and steadied herself. Wind was a steady roar now, and tears streamed from the corners of her eyes.

Looking through the open hatch, she could see the congressional complex coming up below. Too late she remembered Karl was still there, still in the meeting with all the other senators and representatives.

It hurt, but it had to be done. Johnny had given his life for the revolution. Karl had known the risks when he'd agreed to impersonate his father.

She drew the knife from her belt and slit the lines holding the two bundles of missiles in place. Only their weight was keeping them from moving.

"When you near the center of the complex," Shelly called to Lang, "bank to the right."

"Right!" he called back, distantly.

The missiles would slide out the hatch on their little wheeled carts, Shelly thought. And that would be that.

They reached the complex. Below, white marble gleamed; gold leaf shone brightly in the sunlight.

Lang banked the aircar sharply to the right. Shelly set her shoulder against the first bundle of missiles and shoved. It took very little to get it rolling—it slid neatly out the open hatch.

The second bundle followed a moment later. Then Shelly hurtled the other explosives through the hatch one after another.

She didn't watch them fall. "Get us out of here!" she screamed, as she seized the hatch's handle and tried to pull it closed.

The repellers roared. Lang sent the aircar accelerating up and away at a wild pace. Shelly was thrown to the rear of the aircar, hitting her head against the table.

There was a roar like a thousand cannons going off at once. Light, hot and brilliant, flashed through the open hatch for an instant.

Shelly closed her eyes and turned her head. Then the shock wave hit them and the aircar rolled and bucked like a wild animal, careening through the air. There were jarring thuds as debris from the explosion struck the aircar's sides.

In a minute it passed and they were in quiet air again. The repellers sounded different, Shelly noticed. They whined in protest. Slowly the aircar was circling down.

"Lang?" Shelly called. Painfully she got to her hands and knees. She found blood on her face, on her daysuit; her head was bleeding where she'd struck the table. Staggering a bit, she managed to walk. Halfway to the driver's compartment the rope around her middle stopped her. She fumbled at the knots until they were undone, then pushed open the door and went in.

Lang's face was a mess of blood; there was an oozing

cut on his forehead, where he'd struck the control panel. He was also unconscious. The aircar had gone to backup safety measures and was landing in the nearest open area . . . the congressional mall.

The radio was beeping urgently; there was someone trying to reach them.

Shelly ignored the radio. Unstrapping Lang from his shoulder harness, she dragged him back into the passenger compartment. Then she slid into the seat and took the controls.

The repellers felt sluggish, but they responded soon enough. She stabilized their flight and turned them back toward the Sprawl. Only then did she tab on the radio.

"Yes," she said.

The speakers crackled with static. A woman's voice said, "You are instructed to land in area eleven-Afour, pending an official SecurNet investigation into the explosions at the congressional complex."

"Negative," Shelly said. "This is Senator Winston's private aircar. We have an injured man on board. We are en route to a hospital now."

There was a long pause. Then the woman said, "Identity confirmed. Proceed."

"Thank you," Shelly said.

She leaned back. In the rear monitors she could see the congressional complex—or rather, what was left of it. The gold dome was completely gone; of the five marble sides, only two were still standing. The middle of the buildings was a glowing orange pit where fires still roared with the heat of a blast furnace. Nobody could live through that, Shelly thought, not even a senator. Not even Karl.

Only then did she realize what she'd done. But there was no real sense of triumph, though this was what she'd worked and strived for throughout her adult life. Rather, there was a curious sick feeling in her stomach, and she felt as though the world had pretty much collapsed around her.

Johnny was gone. Karl was gone. The Disruption was over and done with. Now her main purpose in life—to destroy congress and all the tyranny it stood for—had been accomplished. What was left?

Behind her, Lang stirred and moaned. It was a good sign, Shelly thought; he wasn't dead. She set the aircar on autopilot and went to see about him.

CONGRESS: MOMENTS AGO, FIFTEEN TERRORIST MIS-
SILES DEMOLISHED THE CONGRESSIONAL COMPLEX
AND KILLED AN ESTIMATED 600 SENATORS AND REPRE-
SENTATIVES. THIS ATTACK FOLLOWED MOMENTS
AFTER THE ANNOUNCEMENT THAT CONGRESS WOULD
CREATE AN EXECUTIVE BRANCH OF GOVERNMENT AND
ASSIGN EXECUTIVE DUTIES TO A NEWLY APPOINTED
PRESIDENT. NO TERRORIST GROUP HAS YET CLAIMED
RESPONSIBILITY, BUT ACCORDING TO SECURNET, PRIME
SUSPECTS ARE SURVIVING MEMBERS OF *THE DISRUP-
TION*, A TERRORIST ORGANIZATION RECENTLY
SMASHED BY SECURNET.

FOR RELATED STORIES, SEE: 1) *THE DISRUPTION—
SMASHED AT LAST* (10878922-C); 2) TERRORISM TODAY
(10926732-B)

–30–

—20—

S HELLY dug out the aircar's firstaid kit and bent to
see about Lang's head wound. As far as she could
tell, it was just a shallow cut—bloody, but not
overly dangerous. As she sprayed on antiseptic, Lang
winced and opened his eyes.

"That hurts!"

"Be thankful. It means you're still alive." She pressed a
skinpatch in place, held it down till it adhered, then let go
and stood, looking critically at her work.

Lang climbed slowly to his feet, touching the skinpatch
gingerly, tracing his wound.

Shelly said, "You'll have a scar, unless you get it treated

at a bodyshop. But that can wait. First we've got to get back to Tech House. Take a seat; the autopilot's set."

He did so, groaning a bit. "Anyone snooping us?" he asked.

"I'll check." Wiping her hands on a roll of gauze, Shelly went back to the driver's compartment and glanced over the various monitors. Nobody seemed to be following them, and no SecurNet or feet vehicles were in sight. She flicked on the security devices. Their aircar wasn't being tracked by radar or laser sights, so she concluded the getaway had been clean. She punched in a different course for Tech House, one less direct, in case someone tried to track them by their course from the complex.

Then, shaking her head, she went back into the passenger compartment. "No sign of SecurNet or the feet. Probably more concerned with the complex right now than routine traffic." She chuckled.

Sitting, she punched up the vid again. Johnny's smiling face looked out from the first of the NewsNet feeds.

It can't be him! she thought, for an instant panicking, images of him somehow faking his death leaping through her mind. *It has to be a recording.* She'd seen him fall, *seen* the shock in his eyes as he died. There wasn't a chance in hell he could still be alive!

Johnny was saying: ". . . and Nexus wishes to welcome you to a fresh era of American democracy—a bright new dawn of freedom across the country. Following the revelation that eighty-five senators and representatives had secretly stolen over seven hundred trillion newdollars from congressional funds, Congress has elected to step down as governing body of the United States of America.

"I am pleased to announce that—by congressional appointment—the new president of the United States is longtime political activist and senatorial adviser Shelly Tracer." Shelly's picture flashed onto the screen.

"You bastard!" Shelly shouted, leaping to her feet. "I don't *want* to be president—"

Lang grinned up at her. "It's a bit late now."

An instant later, Karl's picture appeared. "Congress has also appointed former Senator Sanders Winston as acting vice president. Appointments to the president's cabinet will be announced shortly."

Shelly leaned back. That bit about Karl being vice president confirmed her suspicion about the tape being a recording. Karl was dead, along with the rest of Congress. That she *knew.*

Suddenly her head hurt. Johnny'd made her the goddamn *president*. God, he could make things difficult. How could he have chosen her? What did she know about ruling a country?

Johnny was saying: "—citizens are advised to go on with their work as though nothing had happened.

"The president has announced her first changes already. SecurNet is hereby disbanded. An elite President's Guard will be formed in its place. All members of SecurNet are ordered to report to the east gate SecurNet station at eight hundred tomorrow for reassignment."

The picture faded to black, then cut to a aerial view of the smoldering congressional complex. The voiceover said: "In an unrelated event, terrorists today destroyed the congressional complex, killing an estimated six hundred senators and representatives, including newly appointed Vice President Sanders Winston. Fortunately, the president herself was not injured in the missile attack."

The view cut to a man in char-smeared SecurNet uniform; behind him lay the smoking wreckage of the congressional complex. "We never saw the missiles coming," he said to the camera. "It was a routine meeting, far as I could tell. And then suddenly there was this huge explosion, and the flames—God, the flames were everywhere—"

The feed cut to a man at a NewsNet anchor's desk. He smiled at the camera. "There are no reported survivors of this, the worst terrorist attack on Congress since the Disruption was smashed by SecurNet.

"On the lighter side, SteelAmerica signed a new contract with its programming union to—"

"Shit," Shelly said, downing the volume. She looked at Lang. "I'm the goddamn president!"

"I'm sure Johnny meant himself to be president," he said. "Since he was dead, the techs must have altered his tape to name you in his place."

"Yeah," she mused. That made more sense. Johnny was the one who should have been president, the one who seemed born to the task. With him out of the way, that just left her, since none of the techs could ever make an acceptable president. *Poor Karl.* She looked out the window. *I'm sorry,* she thought. *I didn't mean it for you.*

"What are you going to do?" Lang asked.

"Accept, of course. I see no way out."

"Not that you'd want out," he said.

"Not that I'd want out," she agreed. Now that she thought about it, her being president made a certain amount of sense. She was honest and conscientious enough to try to do a good job. And, too, she believed in democracy the way few others seemed to these days. She'd make sure there were free elections when the time came . . . when the government had been purged of its thieves and cutthroats.

Two hours later, their aircar landed on Tech House's roof. Almost at once there came a flurry of activity outside. When Shelly opened the hatch, she found herself looking out across a crowd of glitterfolk interviewers from the NewsNets: some held still-image cameras, some vids, others microphones. They thrust their equipment into her face and began calling questions all at once.

"What's it like being president?"

"What sort of bathroom soap do you like?"

"How old are you?"

"What do you think of the terrorist attack on Congress?"

Shelly stopped and raised her hands for quiet, looking out across the crowd, trying her best to be sincere as she said: "I was shocked and appalled when I learned about the attack on the congressional complex. Losing so many congressmen is a blow to our whole country. But life goes on, and this is a good time to clean up the corruption in Congress."

Again they shouted questions:

"Where was SecurNet?"

"Why haven't there been any arrests?"

Shelly said, "I assure you, I personally will be looking into the matter. Now, if you'll excuse me, I have work to do. There must be arrests in connection with the thefts of congressional funds."

The glitterfolk called still more questions, incessantly probing, but Shelly ignored them and pushed her way through the crowd. Suddenly Liberator was at her side. He took her elbow and guided her into the elevator, made sure nobody followed, and pushed the down button.

"Who told them I was here?" Shelly said, after the doors had closed.

"I leaked it to the NewsNets," he said.

"Why—"

"It was necessary. For the moment, you must be a media event everywhere you go. People believe everything they see on the NewsNets. If reporters say you have been elected president, and give you such special treatment, then this behavior will be imprinted in the minds of the masses. Because they believe it, it will be so."

"You sound like Johnny now."

"It was his plan originally. And he was always right, you know. That's why so many of us have made it a point to study his writings on social dynamics."

"His—or Gilford's?"

"There is no difference."

The elevator doors opened. Anne Bonny was waiting there with neatly folded red clothes. She thrust them into Shelly's arms. "Put on this uniform," she said. "We've called a NewsNet conference for half an hour from now. Liberator'll go over all th' announcements you've already made and prepare ya to answer th' questions they'll be askin'."

"But—" Shelly started, but Anne Bonny had already entered the lift and pushed the button for another floor. The doors closed.

"This way," Liberator said, taking her elbow again.

She set her feet and refused to budge. "This is all happening too fast. I don't like it."

He sighed. "I don't blame you. Yet it cannot be helped. Johnny had all the plans laid out weeks ago, the course set for us to follow. He was to have been president, not you."

"I figured."

"Now we've had to restructure the whole program. Others are going through the vidtapes, making alterations in Johnny's announcements, naming you as president instead of him; meanwhile, we have to prepare you to take his place. And that means starting with the NewsNet people. Even if you're not quite emotionally ready, it must be done. Would you have Johnny's work all go for naught?"

She shook her head. "No. For now, I'm in your hands . . . do whatever you have to."

He smiled. "Trust us, Shelly. For Johnny."

"For Johnny," she said.

PRESIDENTIAL CONFERENCE: SHELLY TRACER, NEWLY APPOINTED PRESIDENT OF THE UNITED STATES OF AMERICA, HAS CALLED A NEWS/NET CONFERENCE FOR 20:00:00 THIS EVENING. TOPICS TO BE COVERED INCLUDE: 1) THE TERRORIST MISSILE ATTACK ON CONGRESS WHICH RESULTED IN 687 DEATHS; 2) PLANS FOR REBUILDING THE EXECUTIVE BRANCH OF THE GOVERNMENT; 3) PLANS TO RESTRUCTURE CONGRESS FOLLOWING THE REVELATION THAT 85 CONGRESSMEN HAD BEEN STEALING CONGRESSIONAL FUNDS.

-30-

—21—

S HELLY pulled the gold sash tighter around her middle and glanced nervously across the NewsNet vidcrews stationed around the large room. It was her third speech in as many days, and she still found herself as nervous as ever when she faced the vidcameras. The red uniform Anne Bonny had given her—a deep red shirt with insignia she didn't recognize on the sleeve, black pants with red stripes up the legs, and well-polished black boots —gave her an appearance of authority. She liked it. She knew she'd make a favorable impression on everyone who saw her.

The NewsNet crew cued her. She smiled into the camera. "Good evening, my fellow Americans. I am pleased to report that the reorganization of the American government is proceeding at a rapid pace. As your chosen representative, I wish to keep the lines of communication between us both open and honest. Therefore, in the public interest, I announce the newest changes I have ordered:

"The old Congress has now been officially disbanded. Senators and representatives will henceforth be elected by the people, as provided for under the original Constitution of the United States of America. The first elections will be held one month from today. Information will be forthcoming about how and where to vote. If you wish to run for office yourself, the public databanks contain full details on how to register.

"All other governmental agencies, from the court system to the census bureau, are advised to continue with their duties until otherwise instructed.

"My friends, this return to fair, elected government is the beginning of a new golden age for our country—a golden age in which your voices will be heard and your opinions made to count. I urge you to be patient; there are bound to be a few rough spots in our country's reorganization. But in the long run, you and I will both be the better for it. Good night, and good fortune."

The vidcrews cut the camera feeds. It was over.

Shelly found herself sweating, her legs weak, her face hot. She leaned against the podium and grimaced.

"It went well," Liberator said from behind her.

She turned to look at him. "Yeah?"

"I watched it in the other room. The cameras were all angled up at you, and the audio techs lowered your voice and added a few subliminals to make you more authoritative. It was a very impressive presentation, all things considered. I told you the NewsNets liked you. They're doing their best to build you up in the eyes of the masses."

"I know. But I worry. . . ."

"Don't. Now, I have one last duty for you to attend to. There's a senator—perhaps I should say *ex*-senator— waiting to see you in your office. He was one of the thieves; SecurNet caught him trying to slip the border into Canada. He would have been interred with the other seventeen the President's Guard has caught, but he insisted on seeing you. Claimed to have information, actually, that you'd want to hear."

That made her take notice. "What information?"

"He says he won't talk, except to you."

"What's his name?"

"James Ardent."

She started for her office, saying, "I'll see him now." She stopped. "Unless there's something more pressing?"

"Not really."

"Good." She turned and hurried down the corridor.

Four of Shelly's new Presidential Guards were waiting in her office with a handcuffed man. Shelly crossed to her realwood desk—confiscated from Lee Jones's house—and sat, looking James Ardent over. His clothes were dirt-stained but undeniably expensive; he also needed a shave.

"Senator Ardent, Madam President," one of the guards said smugly. "He was caught trying to run the border into Free Canada."

"Indeed." She looked him up and down once more, letting her disdain show. "And what do you have to say to me that's so important, Mr. Ardent?"

Ardent was trembling all over. "Just this," he said. "You're as much a thief as I am—more so, probably, since you're destroying the country. Without Congress, you won't last a month!"

Shelly leaned forward, smiling. "Oh? Pray, go on, sir. You fascinate me."

"Are you blind?" he cried. "Mexico's about to invade Texas. Have you missed the Mexis' troop movements?

And what about the Free Market? Nobody's acknowledged your right to rule. You know why? I'll tell you. Because your government's going to collapse under its own weight. The bureaucracy's mostly gone, or in hiding. Everyone's afraid—"

"Enough," Shelly said. She drew a pistol from one of her desk's drawers and set it in front of her. To the four guards she said, "Get out. Tell Mr. Liberator I wish to see him. *Now.*"

They hustled. When the door had closed, Shelly studied Ardent's face. His skin was pasty; the flabby skin under his jaw trembled as he swallowed.

At last Liberator came in. Shelly smiled at him and said, "Ardent has some questions about our government."

He raised his eyebrows. "Oh?"

"He says Mexico's about to invade Texas."

"There were signs to that effect. The matter has been dealt with, however."

"How?" Ardent demanded.

Liberator looked from Shelly to him and back again. "Do you want me to speak in front of him?"

"Yes."

"Very well." He cleared his throat. "The comandante of Mexico had plans to annex Texas, in that you're quite correct. But our people have been prowling through the public and private databanks of all the major world powers, and it was an easy matter to find the comandante's personal files. They removed certain information that would be most embarrassing to him should it be revealed publicly. He has been informed of the theft and independently verified it. I spoke to him not an hour ago. We have agreed in principle to a new mutual defense treaty, and the details are currently being negotiated by both our aides. The treaty will bring us closer together in the world situation."

"Another point Ardent makes," Shelly said, "is that nobody has yet recognized our government. He says they're waiting for our economic collapse."

"Since our government has only been officially in existence for some three days, a lack of immediate response is hardly a matter of great concern. Some hesitance in recognizing our government was foreseen, of course, since revolutions—even nonviolent ones—are fragile things in their initial moments. However, I see no immediate threats to our stability. Projections show it likely that President Tracer will remain in power for a minimum of seven years before any ready opposition can be mounted—and that's the worst-case scenario.

"Of course, we have made the expected overtures to the president of The Russias, the Brazilian Empire, China, and various ambassadors of other Free Market powers. Mexico has already recognized us; others should too within the week."

"I think that covers all the problems you mentioned," Shelly said to Ardent, voice sweet. "Now, I have some questions for you. First: where do *your* loyalties lie?"

He straightened. "With myself, of course. I readily admit taking the money offered me. Who wouldn't?"

She went on, "You betrayed a solemn, sacred trust given to your family by the people of this country. Such a betrayal is tantamount to treason. And, of course, the penalty for treason from someone in your position could only have one punishment: death."

He swallowed. "Death. Yes, I expected that."

"Should your case reach the Presidential Court, that is."

"You're good," he said, staring at her. "You want something. Money? Influence? You name it, it's yours."

"I'm not greedy," Shelly said. "I just want your loyalty."

"Shelly, no—" Liberator began.

"That's all?" Ardent said, drowning out Liberator's voice.

Shelly said, "I want you to be the vice president."

"No!" Liberator said.

"*Yes!*" Ardent said, even more loudly. "I agree. I'm the man for the job!"

"Why?" Liberator said to her. "Shelly, why?"

Shelly looked at him. "Because he does care about this country, despite the thefts. He warned me about Mexico and the Free Market when he knew he was probably going to be executed anyway. If that isn't loyalty to the United States, I don't know what is."

"Besides that," Ardent said, smiling now, "I have friends. *Many* friends, and in influential places. My being here will lend legitimacy to her government . . . make the transition of power easier to take for many people in the bureaucracy."

"Make the announcements," Shelly said to Liberator. "Work out the details of Ardent's pardon."

"If that's what you truly wish, Shelly."

"It is." She looked at Ardent. "But know this," she said to him, "you'll be watched, and very closely. Try the slightest trick, the slightest betrayal, and you're a dead man."

"Madam President," he said, managing to sound haughty and hurt and sincere all at once, "*my* loyalty is assured."

"Of course," Shelly said. "I expected no less."

Shaking his head, Liberator turned and left. "Fools," Shelly heard him mutter. She smiled.

Ardent took the opportunity to sit down. "You're shrewd," he said. "You've really won, haven't you? Completely. *Utterly.* I never would've thought it possible."

"Yes," she said, looking at him. "Or perhaps you should say *we've* won now." The key to his handcuffs was on her desk. She picked it up and tossed it to him.

Ardent released himself. "I work with the bureaucracy,"

he said. "That was my major job in Congress. In fact, that's why I missed the congressional meeting—I was too busy negotiating a new pay scale with one of the unions. As soon as people heard about the bombing, about you being appointed president, they panicked. Most are trying to cover up the bribes Congress paid them—"

"What?" Shelly demanded.

He laughed. "Don't look so surprised. That's the way things work in the bureaucracy—you want something done fast, you grease the path with newdollars. Reforms like yours scare people used to being bribed. And now that the bureaucracy's scared, the work's not getting done."

"And you can fix that?"

"Of course. As I said, the bureaucracy's my area of expertise."

"Then get to it."

"I'll have to get cleaned up," he said. "May I use your vidphone? I need to let friends know everything's all right now, that they can continue as usual."

"Go ahead." Shelly stood and moved. Ardent took her place behind the desk and began making his calls. Through them all he kept smiling, happy, relieved, and Shelly knew she'd picked the right man to be vice president.

"Congress was running the national mint," Liberator said. "It's now been shut down, pending your review."

A month had passed since she'd become president, and things were still proceeding at a hectic pace. Shelly'd had scarcely a moment to think about anything; Liberator and Anne Bonny and countless other techs she'd scarcely met kept bringing her reports, kept making new policies and new laws, kept dragging her off to make speeches and announcements and goodwill appearances. All of it dragged at her, making her thoughts slow, her movements slower, until she felt as though she were a hundred years old.

"What's the problem this time?" she said with a sigh.

"Banks have been requesting more funds, but the mint has been refusing to issue them. Even various government loans are now being held up. It seems relatives of certain dead congressmen were running the mint, and they pretty well shut things down in protest of the change in power. As I said, they have all been fired, and reorganization is underway. But it will take at least two weeks before money starts flowing again."

"How much do the banks want, total?"

"Several hundred trillion."

"Use the confiscated money."

His eyebrows raised. "That's been earmarked for rebuilding the power of the presidency."

"And what do you think this is?" She shook her head in frustration. If anything, the trust of the banking system was more important than anything else . . . as long as the money kept moving, everything else would, too. And as long as things kept running, the people would be safe, happy. The thought of what would happen if the Sprawl's economy collapsed was enough to make her shudder . . . the looting, the rioting, the famine. . . .

"As you say," Liberator said.

"The mint will pay us back when it's up and running again."

"Perhaps."

"Perhaps it doesn't matter all that much."

Shrugging, Liberator turned and left.

For the first time in what seemed years, Shelly found herself alone in her office with no pressing meetings to attend and no one standing nearby to whisk her off to yet another appointment. She leaned back in her chair and closed her eyes. God, she was tired.

Even so, sleep wouldn't come; her mind kept returning to the Disruption, to Johnny and Karl. Their deaths in particular still gnawed at her insides. They'd sworn to die, if necessary, in the struggle to topple Congress—damn it, she'd sworn the same thing herself! Now that the fight was won, now that their lifelong goal was reached, how could she blame herself for their deaths? Hadn't it been worth it?

Somehow, she didn't know. She almost would've given it all up to see Johnny once more, alive and well, that jack-dumb smile on his face and those infinitely blue eyes. . . .

Angry at herself for being so weak, she sat up and flipped on the vid, scanning the NewsNets. Fires . . . crimes . . . several new appointments to her advisory council . . . and the first twenty elected senators taking office. . . .

She smiled. The world looked good, like a dream born to life. If Johnny had lived to see it come this far, she knew he would've been happy.

There was a knock on the door. "Come," Shelly called.

Anne Bonny entered with a sheaf of papers. She handed them to Shelly.

"What are these?" she asked, leafing through them. Most were written in languages she didn't understand.

"Acknowledgments of our government, an' congratulations, from other countries. China's came in half an hour ago, and after that, th' others flooded in. It's finally happened, Shel—in the eyes of th' world we're now th' legitimate government of th' United States of America!"

Shelly smiled. They'd won, all right. It had been expensive, but they'd won. Johnny would've been happy. If only he'd been here to see it all come to an end. . . .

Rising, she said, "I'll have to make the announcement, of course. And—"

And then what Anne Bonny'd said actually sank in. "We've won," Shelly said, sounding surprised even to herself. She looked at the papers again. Then she tossed them into the air, grinning madly as they rained down around her. She whooped in triumph. "We've goddamn well *won!*"

Epilog

SHE'D been president for almost a year when the urge hit her to call her parents, to talk to them, to see how they were and what they felt about all she'd done. Alone in her chambers, she dialed their number. The vidphone flickered with static for a moment, then her mother answered.

"Hello, Mother."

"Hello, dear. I saw your picture on the NewsNet tonight —you looked charming in that little red costume."

"Mother, I'm the president of this country now."

"That's nice, dear."

"Doesn't that mean anything to you?"

"I'm glad you're no longer associating with riffraff like that Calvin whatever-his-name-was. He wasn't good for you, Shelly. Now, why did you call, dear? You're in need of money, isn't that it? I'll have Daddy wire you—"

Shelly sighed. "No, Mother. I just thought . . . you might want to hear what's happened. . . ." *That you might be proud of me,* she thought.

"Of course I want to know, dear. I've always interested in anything you and your sisters do."

"Thank you, Mother," Shelly said softly. "Goodbye."

"Goodbye, Shelly. Love you."

"Love you, too, Mother." She severed the connection and leaned back. It didn't seem to matter to her mother that she'd become president. She'd hardly noticed. In fact, none of the masses had missed a step on their treadmill since Congress fell. It hurt to realize success could also be such failure. She'd wanted to awaken the people, free them from tyranny. Now that they were free, none had noticed.

Or perhaps they were never really that enslaved. Had she ever stopped and *looked* at the world about her? Ever seen the problems the people suffered?

Feeling empty inside, she stood and wandered to the far wall, then tabbed off the mural. The wall became a glass window looking down eighty stories onto the streets. From this height the people below seemed like gnats scurrying about on some model of a city. These teaming masses were the ones she'd fought and won for, she told herself; she couldn't let herself forget it. If she did, would she be any better than Congress?

She had an odd urge to go down and see the people she governed, to walk among them, to mingle with them and hear and see and feel what they were doing. To be part of them once more.

She went to her bedroom and took off her uniform. Her old clothes were still there, and she picked out a black daysuit and slipped it on. Using makeup, she changed her face, darkening her hair and eyes, brightening her lips, accentuating the curve of her cheekbones. It was easy to fall back into childhood routines of dressup, and soon she was disguised, no longer recognizable as the president. On the street she'd be just another burber out sleazing in the Sprawl.

She opened the side door and went out, ignoring the startled expressions on her two bodyguards' faces.

"Madam President?" one said, moving to follow.

She waved him away. "I won't need you," she said.

"But you can't go out there alone—"

"I did it every day of my life for ten years!" she snapped. "Are you telling me I've forgotten how to walk down the street?"

"No, no," he said quickly. "It just . . . well . . . it doesn't seem proper, somehow. What if someone attacks you? The streets are a dangerous place if you don't know what you're doing. There are terrorists—"

She remembered the airheads in the skyeye bar, remembered the catmen she'd fought. If they knew half of what she'd done in her life. . . .

Suppressing a smile, she said, "Let me worry about what's proper."

"At least let us know how long you'll be gone. Mr. Liberator'll skin us if you don't come back—"

"I'll be back. Just go on as though I were still inside my office. That's all. I'll be back before I'm missed. Trust me."

"Yes, Madam President." Both guards saluted, then reluctantly returned to their place beside her door.

It was a simple matter to take a lift down to the street level, then to hop a transit platform fifty blocks upSprawl to one of the glitzier shopping streets.

She wandered among the crowds of glitterfolk and burbers, listening to their chatter, watching their bright, distracted eyes, searching for something—she didn't know quite what.

Streeters lounged in all the doorways below the neon

signs, some glitterdressed, most not. She noticed them watching her as she meandered past. Perhaps they thought she might be an easy tag. Perhaps they just wondered who she was. She wasn't sure she knew herself.

Among the streeters was a young man sitting alone. Something about him reminded her of Johnny: the tilt of his head, the way the blue and red of the neon lights reflected in his eyes.

She paused and nodded to him. When he nodded back, she climbed the steps and sat, too.

"You lookin'?" he said.

"Just for talk."

He laughed. "That's a new'n. Nev' heard it 'fore."

"Will you talk to me?"

"Yeah, sure. Kinky, y'know?"

"Yeah," she said, leaning back, staring at the glitterfolk as they strutted past in their brilliant costumes. "I'm feeling . . . I don't know. Lost. Lonely. I want to hear about everything—about life and love, death and taxes. *Everything.*"

He slid closer to her, put his arm around her, turned her head, and kissed her lips. His touch was soft, gentle, plying. Shelly gazed into his blue, infinitely blue eyes and could not pull away.

Finally the streeter drew back. Laughing, he said, "You really wanna talk, don't ya?"

"Yeah. Tell me about life."

"What's there to tell? Money flows out more'n in these days. Times're slow."

"Are you happy?"

"I don't know."

"Love. Tell me about love."

He looked into her eyes. "I could love you."

"What's the best thing that's ever happened?"

"To me?"

"To the world."

He shrugged. "Congress gettin' blown, you know? No more SecurNet hassles."

"Don't you like the government?"

He glanced left-right-left, then grinned and shook his head. "Spies ev'where, y'know. The President's Guard're tough, always listening."

"Maybe I'm one."

"Nah . . ." He giggled. "Too weird. You see someone like SecurNet ever just talk?"

"What about the president?"

"I dunno . . . nev' had her." He grinned wider. His teeth were perfect, like Johnny's had been.

"She ever do anything for you?"

"You ask a lotta questions."

"I'm a curious person. Did you vote?"

"What for?"

"Senators. Representatives. You know."

"Congress?"

"Yeah. Congress."

He shrugged. "Why bother?"

"Maybe it's your right as a citizen to vote. Maybe you should take interest in the world around you. Maybe—"

He touched her lips with two soft fingers. "Slicker down. There's only one person here 'bouts runnin', News-Nets said. So why bother?"

"Next time—"

He shrugged. "Same guy'll run. Congressional family, y'know? They're the ones who work things. And even if he lost, someone just like him'd win. They're all the same."

"You could run for senator," she said.

His eyes widened. "Me? Radical, that." Then he laughed. "Wouldn't help. Nothin' ever changes here. The taxes are the same, the people are the same. So there's a president 'stead of a Congress. All the same anyways! And who cares? Gotta eat first. That's what's important, y'know?" Chuckling, he leaned back on his elbows. But there was something wistful in his expression now.

Shelly found herself agreeing with what he'd said. *It never changes. Just the faces. Just the names. Replace Congress with a president and it's still the same.*

"So you'd like the president?" she whispered.

"Why not?"

"Silly boy." She drew him to her, kissing *him* this time, her lips hot on his. If she closed her eyes she could feel Johnny kissing her, Johnny's hands caressing her. She could lose herself and drift in time to the simpler days when revolutions could work and dreams and ideals still meant something. Then the fight could be won and all could end happily.

The people were worried about the important things: food, shelter, sex, day-to-day survival. They didn't care about politics because politics was remote, legendary as an eagle, a game for the time-rich. For a second, Shelly thought of herself. She'd pushed herself from the idle distractions of her class and found herself adrift without purpose. So she'd played the power game and she'd won . . . an empty honor.

Nothing has really changed, she thought. But when she closed her eyes and he kissed her, it was magic, it was dreams, and she could always win in the end.

Society has always chosen certain people to be the driving force behind the cultural currents of humanity. Whether for good or bad, History must decide. I do not envy these leaders the tasks they have had to perform. Rather, I pity them. Power is a terrible burden.

—Shelly Tracer